THE LIE DESTROYER

Bobby Carson is proud of his lying expertise. His scientist father uses him as a guinea pig for a machine which destroys his ability to be dishonest, but has unhappy social consequences. Soon criminals begin exploiting the possibilities of a world without lies in a society built upon sham and pretence. And Scotland Yard, hampered by its own guilty secrets, cannot stem the tide of blackmail . . . until Dr. Carson, the creator of the Lie Destroyer, again steps into the scene . . .

JOHN RUSSELL FEARN

THE LIE DESTROYER

Complete and Unabridged

LINFORD
Leicester

First published in Great Britain

First Linford Edition
published 2010

British Library CIP Data

Fearn, John Russell, *1908 – 1960.*
    The lie destroyer.- -(Linford mystery library)
    1. Truthfulness and falsehood- -Fiction.
    2. Discoveries in science- -Fiction.
    3. Science fiction. 4. Large type books.
    I. Title II. Series
    823.9'12–dc22

    ISBN 978–1–84782–979–5

1

The Experiment

The one thing that mainly troubled Dr. Mark Carson, the celebrated scientist, was that his son was a most unconscionable liar. Bobby Carson, aged eighteen, was in most respects a normal youth. He behaved as most youths do and in many ways as most youths should not. The trouble was his persistent penchant for lying. He even seemed to glory in it. It had been evident since the earliest days of his childhood, right from the day that he had been able to speak, he had always seemed to choose a lie in favour of the truth.

So far this had not got him into any serious trouble, but there was no telling when it would and all the psychiatrists and so-called mental experts who had examined him could find no particular brain reason why he should behave like this — and yet he did. There could be only one explanation: he just loved lying.

It was because Dr. Mark Carson was a scientist that he decided something ought to be done about it. He had got to cure his son of this weakness, nay, this evil. So it was that Mark Carson went to work with charts and plans. He consulted other experts in the field of science, notably those versed in neuroscience; he also had many consultations with brain surgeons, the sum total of which proved to Carson that the flaw in his son's makeup lay in one particular portion of his brain. It was not that Bobby was unique in any way. There was nothing unusual about his brain. His father discovered that every human being has this particular formation in the brain, which in some cases is extremely overdeveloped — or hypertrophied to use the scientific expression. And in other cases so unusually mature that the pure criminal results.

However, Dr. Carson's main idea after consulting these various experts and studying his own diagrams was to find a way to deal with this particular portion of the brain. If various vibrations could be used in therapeutics to reduce this or that disorder, this or that muscular reaction — then why not a vibration which could be used upon the brain? So to this end Dr. Carson devoted his energies. He drew numerous plans and designs, calling upon his considerable scientific knowledge to develop them to the full.

He was, in actual profession, a scientist in the employ of the Government. His work was chiefly research into rare metals, but from a beneficent government he did not draw enough money to own the tremendous home in which he lived together with its annexed laboratories. No, this was the outcome of various inventions, which he had created on the side. He had produced many marvellous devices chiefly for the benefit of the housewife. Indeed one journalist had harked back to the old days of radio and called him 'Housewives' Choice'. Here, though, was serious business. A method of vibration that would control the brain. It was no easy task and he spent every spare moment at it, during which time somebody cheerfully went on his way as the exact opposite of George Washington.

There came a day, however, when at last Dr. Carson had the main basic outlines of his invention and felt confident enough of it to explain the details to his wife.

His wife, Ethel, was anything but a scientist. She was a quiet, good-natured, serious woman, intellectual to a degree, some fifteen years younger than Carson and therefore not so much given to long moods in introspective silence as he was. She tried to understand his scientific inclinations, which was no easy task, and where she failed Carson made no attempt to reprove her. He knew that he lived in a world of his own, but he also knew — though he doubted if Ethel did — that he could not continue to live in this world without her at his side. She meant everything to him, and was the kingpin about which his life revolved.

'You see, Ethel,' he explained one evening when they were seated in the lounge together after dinner. 'I have been thinking for a long time about Bobby's tendency to lie. It is not a nice thing. In fact it is an immensely evil thing. Here and there a little fib doesn't mean anything, particularly if it gets you out of a difficulty. The limit comes when one lies consistently just for the sake of it, which unhappily is just what Bobby does.'

Ethel did not say anything; indeed she could not. She knew Bobby's tendency and though she always sought to protect him in everything, she could not do so in this instance. She sat looking at her husband — he was a short, bald-headed, earnest little man with keen eyes over-shadowed by bushy brows. He was looking at her in that intent solemn way he had when he poised so to speak over the edge of a great revelation.

'Yes,' Ethel agreed after a long pause. 'I know Bobby is not exemplary in the matter of truthfulness, but there is nothing we can do about it. After all, Mark, we have tried everything. Psychia-trists, doctors, his school teachers, even we ourselves have done what we can to make him behave normally, He just doesn't and I can't understand where he gets it from. I'm sure I'm no greater liar than anybody else. I admit I have told a fib maybe here and there, even a white lie, but I've never indulged in a torrent of black ones.'

Carson cleared his throat a little.

'It is not so much a case of where Bobby gets it from, my dear, as a case of how we are going to stop it. And I believe I can stop it, scientifically!'

Ethel looked unconvinced.

'Just what do you mean by that?' Immediately her mother instincts were on the defensive. 'How can you possibly scientifically stop a person from lying? I mean, lying is an untouchable sort of thing, like thought. You can't do anything to a thought except perhaps by a lot of useless talking and so-called education.'

'I'm not dealing in anything so complicated as thought and mental psychology,' Carson replied. 'When I say deal with it scientifically, I mean I have devised an instrument, which by vibration, can so control the brain that it will destroy the area responsible for lying.'

Ethel visibly started.

'Destroy!' she echoed. 'What in the world do you mean by that? You're not going to do anything to Bobby that may destroy part of his brain! Just what are you thinking of?'

'I'm thinking of the future.' Carson gave a moody glance. 'One day Bobby will sure enough get himself into a fearful jam with this lying of his. For his own sake it's got to be stopped and I'm going to do it. Don't be alarmed my dear, there's nothing dangerous about it. Either the experiment succeeds, or else it fails and nobody will be any the wiser, least of all Bobby. It simply consists of releasing a vibration that will affect the particular area of the brain responsible for lying.

'I do not expect you to understand the formation of a brain. In fact only an expert could do so. But I know enough about it to know that it is built up in layers, that it is a mass of cells, neurons, ganglia and similar scientific terms, but certain areas are responsible for truthfulness or otherwise. It lies just behind the subconscious region. This vibration that I'm speaking of can penetrate the skullbone and actually affect the brain itself. What it does is to neutralise the nervous stimulation of the cells directly responsible for one's conduct, which includes lying, of course.'

'To me,' Ethel said seriously, 'it all sounds diabolical, and I'd much rather you didn't do anything at all about it. Anyway you're not a brain surgeon. Why don't you stay, so to speak, in your own back yard?'

'Because, Ethel, Bobby is in my back yard and yours. I repeat, there is nothing to fear. Under the influence of the vibration he will feel nothing more than if he were standing in a ray of sunlight. In fact, not even that. For a ray of sunlight is warm, and this will not be in the least appreciable to him. In fact, if I can arrange it, he will not even be aware that I am doing anything at all.'

'That,' Ethel remarked, 'would be far better. I, personally, would not blame Bobby if he smashed your precious instruments completely if he discovered what you were up to.'

Carson gave a moody glance.

'Tell me something, Ethel. Why do you defend Bobby to such an extent? You cannot possibly agree with the way he lies.'

'No,' Ethel agreed. 'I do not agree with that, but he is still my son, and that, to say the least of it, is one reason why I don't like him tampered with.'

'He is also my son,' Carson reminded her, 'and I'll either make him an honourable boy or know the reason why. However, at the moment, this instrument of mine is only on the drawing board. It will take me perhaps three weeks to make the thing complete, and then I intend to experiment and see what happens.'

Ethel reflected for several moments. Then she said:

'Are you making Bobby the first subject or are you going to try it on somebody else first — yourself for instance?'

'I could not possibly try it on myself because there is too much control needed. I must have a separate subject. In any case if it does not work, as I said before, all we have to show is a failure. No injury, no knowledge of what has happened, no anything. Bobby can just as easily be the first subject as anybody else.'

'And will the effect be temporary or permanent? I mean is it just for the time being while the effect lasts, like novocaine when you go to a dentist, and you get the most horrible after-effects in time, or — ?'

'It will be permanent,' Carson interrupted. 'Once the particular area has been dealt with it can never function again. It is complete destruction.'

'But how will it affect his behaviour generally? Will he become incredibly angelic, or totally changed in his nature, or what? It all sounds to me such a horrible dabbling with the normal processes of life.'

'He will not be changed in any appreciable degree,' Carson replied. 'The only thing different about him will be, that he will be completely incapable of telling a lie. There are also the broader implications to this idea; everybody in this world, I'm convinced, with the exception perhaps of a few saints in the past or maybe even the fabulous George Washington, has at some time or other

10

told a lie in order to escape some difficult predicament. Anybody who says he has not is a liar thereby for saying such a thing. Imagine then, if this idea of mine could be broadened, if the instrument could be used to deal, not with a single individual, as in the case of Bobby, but with the entire section of the population. I wonder now what would a world without lies be like?'

'Ruinous,' Ethel replied promptly. 'You just think it over carefully, Mark. Detach yourself from your scientific speculations and consider the world as though through a microscope. I do so sometimes, just for the fun of it. You will find that all society is built up on sham, pretence, hypocrisy, lies and deceit. Even in the finest of us there is some form of treachery . . . At least I have yet to find any particular part of the community where it does not exist. Anybody with a frank nature will admit that society is built up on false pretences. If you made everything truthful, I don't see how things could operate at all. I mean,' Ethel continued, stumbling for words, 'if people said outright what was the actual truth about any situation at any given moment, they would immediately become the most unpopular beings on the face of the Earth.'

Carson chuckled. 'Yes, my dear, I believe you're right! Oh, well, I won't endeavour to extend my possibilities of my idea for a while, but I will certainly concentrate on Bobby and see what the result is. And I repeat,' he added, getting to his feet, 'there is absolutely nothing to fear. As his mother I respect your feelings in the matter, but you may be assured that I don't intend to go beyond the bounds of reason.'

With that he shambled out of the lounge, and silently closed the door.

Lost in thought he went along the broad corridor that led to the rear of the house and the annexe in which his laboratory was situated. Here, in a modest array, were all of the many scientific instruments used by him in the pursuit of his various sidelines, and particularly in the creation of those amazing inventions that had done so much to make the lot of the housewife easier. But right now Carson was not interested in the lessening of the house-wife's load. It was his son that was absorbing him, the son who was a liar and who must be made truthful . . .

It was about this time that the young man who had started such a train of scientific thought was seated with a group of his friends in the Argos Café in the centre of the city. He was a well-built, handsome youth, with dark hair and blue eyes after the fashion of his mother, and most charming feature of all was his infectious smile. Probably it was this that had enabled him to lie with such ease without arousing anybody's suspicions.

Nobody ever felt inclined to question Bobby. If they did he always laughed it off with an impudent grin. In the main other young men liked him and most of the girls adored him. Particularly the one now seated next to him. Betty Foster, who, rather like many of the girls of her time, was very sophisticated. Or at least she imagined she was. What the elders thought was another matter.

'What,' she asked, 'did you call all of us

here together tonight for, Bobby? I mean there isn't much point in us just sitting around looking at each other, is there? Had you some special reason?'

'A very special reason,' Bobby assured her, patting her hand as it lay on the tablecloth beside him. 'Not only are we all going to have a little supper together here, but I wanted to tell you that I have managed to get the boss to lend me the Rolls for the weekend. So that we can all go down to Franton and have a good time.'

The others looked at him in astonishment, their brows raised.

'You mean,' one of the young men exclaimed, astonished, 'that you actually managed it? How on Earth did you ever do that?'

There was good reason for his enquiry, for Bobby's employer was a hard-fisted, Throgmorton Street financier. He had never been known to lend anything and certainly not to give away anything. That Bobby had managed to get him to loan even his car was the most extraordinary thing ever.

'Oh, it was simple enough,' Bobby said, shrugging. 'I simply told him that down in Franton there is a possible client worth many millions whom I believe I can draw into the Stock and Share broking net. That pleased the old man immensely, but, as I pointed out, I probably could not use the right approach if I went IN the ordinary way by train, with a suitcase in my hand, looking like any Tom, Dick or Harry. The thing to do was to use a car and look really high up in the world and then use my influence.'

'And on the pretext of that he agreed?' Betty asked

'He did. After all, why not? I have managed to swing many a deal for him purely by my personality. So, of course, he sees no reason why I cannot swing another deal.'

'And is there such a person in Franton?' one of the other girls asked. Bobby grinned widely.

'Not to my knowledge, but one story is as good as another. I can always say that I failed to make the grade, return the car, and that's that.'

'I don't quite like it,' Betty Foster looked uneasy. 'Just suppose we all got to Franton and then your boss happened to turn up to see if he could help with the deal? I wouldn't put it past him.'

'He won't go anywhere near Franton,' Bobby said flatly. 'I've got it all worked out. We'll leave late Saturday afternoon. I shall send a message to him before we go, sent by way of a friend in Edinburgh, asking my boss to go up to Edinburgh to clinch a deal. He'll fall for it, but of course he'll only find the whole thing is a hoax when he gets there. He won't be able to trace that to me because he has been hoaxed many times before. He'll simply put it down to another of those things.'

Bobby relaxed and smiled thoughtfully. 'There's such a lot that you can get in this world by just using your noodle,' he explained. 'It doesn't matter whether it's a straight story or a crooked one, just as long as it serves its purpose.'

'I think it's positively wonderful,' Betty Foster said in admiration, with a starry-eyed glance, at which Bobby gave her a gentle hug. 'Tell me,' she continued, 'what do you think of this hat of mine?'

'I think it's superb,' Bobby lied frankly. 'I like the way it tilts. I like its ridiculous size, and even more do I like the girl under it.' The last part of his sentence was quite correct, the earlier part was exactly contrary to his real opinion. He reflected that he had never seen such an atrocious-looking arrangement on any girl's head. It reminded him of a cabbage with a blue hatpin stuck through it.

'Well, that being that,' one of the youths said, 'all we have to do is to make the necessary arrangements to go down to Franton on Saturday.'

'That's it,' Bobby confirmed, nodding.

'Then what do we do now?' Betty asked. 'We don't continue to sit here and have some supper; and then go home, surely. What about a dance?'

'Why not,' Bobby agreed, shrugging. So a dance it was, and at something approaching twenty minutes to one Bobby returned home. It was unusually late even for him and he expected trouble. He expected it even more when he found his father and mother had not yet gone to bed, but were in the lounge waiting for him.

His mother came forward quickly, grasping his arm as she approached.

'Bobby, at last. We were beginning to wonder what on earth had happened to you.'

'Why?' he asked, grinning. 'Surely I'm old enough to look after myself? Nineteen next birthday, don't forget!'

'We're not forgetting,' Carson said briefly. 'Confine yourself to one a.m. as the deadline. I don't like you rambling about in the small hours of the morning. Where have you been?'

'Oh, out with the gang to a late dance. It finished later than we expected.'

'So it would appear,' Carson commented with a cold glance.

'Oh, stop fussing me,' Bobby protested. 'You've never done it before, why start now? And I've been this late many a time before, dad, and you've never said anything.'

'I know, but I think it's time I put my foot down.'

Carson reflected for a moment, then: 'Have you had supper?'

'Yes. We had it at the Argos Café in town. Nothing more I need so I may as well go to bed.'

With a vaguely puzzled look that both his parents should have taken the trouble to see him come home, Bobby turned towards the door, then his father's voice stopped him.

'Just a minute, Bobby. Come here.'

Bobby turned, surprised, and came slowly back across the lounge.

'This, Bobby, is going to surprise you,' his father said slowly. 'Just sit down a moment. Your mother and I have waited up for you specially tonight. Not to see you in or to make sure that you're perfectly all right, but to explain a proposition to you. At least I am going to, and your mother insisted on being present at the same time. That's it, sit down.'

Bobby slowly obeyed, settling on the settee. He gave his mother a wondering glance and received from her a fond look, just as though he were still only two years old.

'Well, dad, what is it?' he asked somewhat sleepily. 'I've had a pretty exhausting time at the dance hall, if it's anything that will keep, I'd sooner discuss it tomorrow.'

'This won't keep.' Carson gave him a level look. 'It concerns, to come straight to the point, your tendency to lies.'

'Oh, that again!' Bobby relaxed and yawned behind his hand.

'I've decided,' Carson said, 'to cure you of that trouble. I could have done it secretly; indeed I was going to do it secretly, but your mother insisted that you be consulted first. Since you are to be the patient I suppose there is a certain logic in what she says.'

Bobby sat up again slowly. 'Dad, what in the world are you talking about?'

'I'm talking about a scientific method of curing your untruthfulness. Since you have individual rights in the matter it is for you to say whether I should do it or not. Just as a doctor would ask his patient if the patient agrees to such-and-such a treatment. It comes to this — ' Carson sat down quickly. 'Are you willing to have your untruthfulness cured?'

'Well,' Bobby said slowly rubbing his chin, 'that all depends. In some cases my adaptability for lies comes in very useful. If I found I hadn't got it I might get into some of the most dreadful spots.'

'Yes, maybe so. But you must surely admit that honesty is a far better policy than lies?'

'It's a matter of opinion,' Bobby said thinking. 'Anyway, what's all this about? Have you got some new-fangled psychiatric treatment or something? If it's anything like those old fools that started prodding around and asking me a lot of ridiculous questions some years ago, forget it. I want nothing to do with boys like that any more.'

'No, it's nothing like that,' Carson said. 'I have devised a scientific instrument, probably the first of its kind in the world, which, reacting upon the brain of a person — it could be anybody, but in this case I wish it to be you — it can destroy all tendency to dishonesty, lying, deceit or anything. Do you understand?'

'No, I don't understand!' Bobby

replied frankly. 'Am I expected to at this early hour in the morning?'

Carson gave a hurt look. 'No, I suppose not. Well, since you're no scientist, Bobby, I'll just tell you briefly that the machine operates on a vibratory principle. What it does is to completely neutralise the portion of the brain responsible for lying. It will make the person under treatment incapable of telling a lie. The treatment is brief and certain. It takes no more than three minutes to perform the operation.'

'It sounds intriguing,' Bobby admitted. 'But supposing something goes wrong? I've no particular wish to depart this life at present. Particularly as I'm going down to Franton with the gang at the weekend.'

'You're what?' his mother asked in surprise, starting.

'Going down to Franton. There's no reason why not. We've been to that little hotel there many a time in the past.'

'Yes, I know,' his mother agreed, 'but that was during the summer months, a very different thing. Franton, as I recall it, is a sleepy one-eyed seaside little town somewhere in Kent. What on earth do you and the rest of your friends expect to do there in the middle of November?'

Bobby grinned widely. 'Oh, there are plenty of things we can do. The point is we want to be together for a while, all young people at the same time. In case you don't know it, mother, and this applies to you as well, father, parents can be a confounded nuisance sometimes. Anyway,' Bobby asked indignantly, 'what's wrong with the idea?'

'Oh, nothing, I suppose,' his mother shrugged. 'I just wish that you didn't go about with those boys and girls quite so much. They're hardly your type.'

'Maybe not, but Betty Foster's all right,' Bobby replied, winking. 'And it means we can have a bit of fun away from the city. I've got it all figured out. I'm going to borrow Mr. Henshaw's Rolls and we're all going to pile into it and go down together.'

Carson looked up. 'You're going to borrow Mr. Henshaw's Rolls?' he repeated, astonished. 'Why, has he agreed to lend it to you?'

'Certainly he has. Not exactly for the

reason I intend, but I gave him a good enough excuse and that's all that matters.'

'In other words, lies again?' Carson asked.

'Oh, for heavens' sake!' Bobby got up irritably, 'why do you have to keep rubbing it into me, dad, and you too, mum, if it comes to that? I've got my own way of living. Why on earth do you have to be so saintly about everything?'

'It's not a question of being saintly,' Carson said curtly. 'We just happen to live up to what we believe is an honest standard and we don't intend that our son should do otherwise. To get back to the point. This invention of mine, are you willing that I should try it on you?'

'Sure,' Bobby replied grinning. 'I'll try anything once, but I'd like to gamble it won't work.' He hesitated, his grin fading and a troubled look coming into his blue eyes.

'That's a point,' he said. 'Suppose it doesn't work? What happens to me? Do I go out like a light or something? Do you want me to sign a letter of exoneration or something, in case things go wrong?'

'That will not be necessary,' Carson told him, 'and I don't like your tone either, Bobby. The invention is absolutely foolproof. First thing in the morning before you go to business I'll try it out and you can see for yourself.'

'Why wait till first thing in the morning?' Bobby asked. 'We seem to be clowning around now when we ought to be in bed. Is there any reason why we can't try it now?'

'Yes, there's the very simple reason that it's not yet completed. Originally I thought it would take me three or four weeks to complete it, but since then I have discovered that it merely requires the conversion of an ordinary radio amplifier to do the trick. That means that an enormous amount of preliminary work has been cut out and by simple adjustment of wiring I can produce the effect I want even in a few hours. If you are willing to undergo the treatment, as you have said you are, I can have the equipment ready by tomorrow morning.'

'By working on it all night?' Bobby asked; incredulous.

'Yes, if need be. I don't want you to change your mind, my boy.'

'Personally,' Bobby's mother broke in, 'I don't think you should have anything to do with the idea, Bobby. There's something unnatural about it to my mind. Your father's a scientist and doesn't see anything wrong in it, but I do as an ordinary individual. It's tampering with things which would be better left alone.'

'I don't mind tampering with anything so long as it is entertaining,' Bobby replied shrugging. 'All right, dad, first thing in the morning it is. I'm sorry you have to work all night on account of the fact that I tell untruths so easily, but if you want to give yourself some hard work you can't blame me. So, goodnight and good luck!'

He turned and left the lounge, closing the door sharply behind him. Carson reflected then presently he turned to meet the eyes of his wife.

'That settles that,' he said quietly.

'Yes, to a certain extent,' she agreed. 'I personally thought he would never agree which shows that perhaps I don't understand him quite as well as I thought I did. It would seem it's no use me saying anything more, Mark, so I suppose you'll go ahead with it?'

'Most definitely I will, but I assure you that you're still worrying needlessly.' Carson came forward and patted his wife's shoulder affectionately. 'You go on to bed, my dear, I'll follow on later if there's time. Otherwise I shall go on working right through the night. I've got the chance of Bobby being a willing subject and I don't intend to lose it. You see, I would run into quite a number of difficulties if I had to perform this treatment surreptitiously.'

'Oh, you would?' Ethel looked surprised. 'But I thought you intended to do it secretly in any case?'

'In the first instance I did, yes. But I find now that the vibration is so minute that it would be impossible to locate or rather to focus it accurately without the co-operation of the person concerned. Therefore this acquiescence on Bobby's part is all I need, and believe me, I'll get the result.'

And knowing her husband as she did, Ethel was pretty sure that he would. And she was right! At eight o'clock the following morning, Bobby came into the laboratory freshly shaven and dressed to find his father still at work on his apparatus. He was driving home the last screws. He looked tired, was unshaven, and in his shirtsleeves. He glanced up as Bobby entered.

'Time to put the blinds up, dad,' Bobby said, snapping the switch which set the shades rattling up into their sockets. 'In case you don't know it, a new day has dawned. Or what there is of it. It's November, drizzling and cold as blazes. Now do you want the experiment before breakfast or after? I hope you say after because I'm darned hungry.'

'Preferably before, Bobby. It doesn't really signify whether you have eaten or not, but from the medical standpoint it would be better if you have this treatment on an empty stomach.'

'I was afraid of that,' Bobby sighed. 'Well, what do I have to do? Do you want me to strip or anything? Maybe I should have asked you that first then I wouldn't have needed to go to the trouble of dressing.'

His father did not answer immediately. He finished screwing the cowling of his peculiar-looking apparatus into place and laid down the driver carefully. Turning, he looked at his son with tired eyes.

'There's no need to strip or anything like that, my boy, this is a brain operation. All you have to do is to sit in that chair over there.'

Bobby glanced to it, nodded, and with a cheerful smile seated himself as requested.

'All set?' he enquired.

'Not quite.' His father moved across to him and for the next five minutes he was busy positioning his son until at last he had him exactly as he wanted him. This done he moved back to the peculiar apparatus on the bench and swung it round on a miniature turntable. After that he fiddled about with a variety of switches and adjusted a complicated-looking lens on the front of the apparatus.

Bobby watched all this with interest,

that roguish smile still hanging round his lips.

'Looks just like a glorified enlarging camera,' he commented finally. 'Can it take photographs as well?'

His father looked irritated.

'Bobby, I could forgive your jocular attitude if this were not such a serious business. You don't seem to realise that I'm about to perform on you an experiment which has never been performed on anybody before.'

'I know,' Bobby looked rather anxious. 'That's what's worrying me. No reflection on you, dad, you're a first-class scientist, as so many newspapers acknowledge, but I suppose there has to be a first time for everything. I'm just wondering whether you did right in choosing me.'

'Nobody else I could choose,' his father told him. 'And nobody else more appropriate to the subject. After all, Bobby, though you are my son you're quite the most consummate liar that I ever knew. So, let's see what can be done. Now, just relax, that's all.'

'Right!' Bobby made himself more comfortable and stretched his elegantly-trousered legs out in front of him. 'How's this? You getting my profile nicely?'

'I'm not a photographer,' his father retorted dryly, 'and in any case I don't want your profile; it's the back of your head that I'm interested in. At this moment my guide ray is focussed exactly upon the area that I require.'

'Guide ray! What's that?'

'It's just an ordinary pencil of light like a pilot light, which shows me the area I wish to deal with. Now sit perfectly motionless whilst I make the necessary adjustments.'

Bobby did as he was told, still grinning to himself, and in his mind's eye thinking, not of the experiment, but of the delectable charms and curves of Betty Foster, whilst his father doggedly turned the focussing lens of his vibratory projector until at last he had it to his liking.

'Right,' his father said finally. 'I think we're ready. Are you ready too, Bobby?'

'Shoot father, I am not afraid,' Bobby

hesitated for a moment, 'or is that rather inappropriate considering that it was George Washington who said it?'

'It was not George Washington my boy, it was William Tell — but no matter. It was George Washington who said: 'I cannot tell a lie, father, I did it with my little hatchet'. 'Pon my word, boy, I cannot imagine why I spent such a fortune upon your education. However, here we go.'

Carson snapped over the switch. From the blades of the switch there sprang a brief coruscation of sparks that instantly died away. The vibratory instrument whirred gently and then settled down into a gentle humming. From the projecting, snout-like lens of the instrument, nothing was visibly emanating. There was no beam, no coloured light, no anything. There hardly could be since it was vibration and not in the visible scale. The only proof that Carson had of its presence at all was the recording on the meter dials, and it showed him that the vibration was being projected at maximum.

Bobby just sat as he was, motionless, gazing in front of him. He did not feel anything, not so much as a twinge, no sense of warmth, no sense of movement whatsoever. He just went on thinking about Betty Foster. The more he thought about her the more he smiled.

'Just remain motionless,' his father said after a moment or two, 'this won't be very long now. One and a half minutes have gone, another one and a half should see the finish.'

'After which I tell no more lies?' Bobby asked, his voice cynical in spite of himself.

'So I hope.' Carson kept his eyes on his watch, deflecting them only for a moment to glance at the meters. 'We shall soon see.'

The seconds passed swiftly, then at last Carson pulled out the switch and the humming ceased. Bobby relaxed even further into his chair and then glanced round over his shoulder.

'Have we finished?' he asked.

'Definitely, my boy. Now we come to the great moment. Did the experiment succeed or not?'

'Sounds like a serial play,' Bobby grinned. 'I can hardly wait to know the answer.'

'Oh, that's easily settled.' His father studied him carefully. 'Tell me something, Bobby. If I were to ask you what you really think of me, your father, what would be your answer?'

'Well now,' Bobby rubbed his chin. 'I should say that you're a very clever scientist; you're a little stuffy in your outlook; you haven't entirely shaken off the Victorian era. Well, taking it all round at heart, a good sort, but — er — you've forgotten the day when you were young. You expect everybody else to behave just as you do now. Anything else?'

'That is your absolute opinion?' Carson asked.

'A genuine opinion, yes.'

'You're not saying it just to please me?' Carson asked.

'Certainly not. Just giving you an unvarnished answer.'

'I see. Well, I'm glad to know the absolute truth about myself. For that is definitely what it should be.'

Bobby gave a start. 'Why, come to think of it, it is the absolute truth about you. It is exactly how I feel towards you.' He began to look astonished. 'I can't think why I said that about you being stuffy. I must have a hell of a sight more nerve than I thought I had.'

Carson smiled a little. 'It's not a question of nerve, my boy. It's a question of inability to tell anything but that which is true. Now, why are you going down to Franton on Saturday?'

'Well, I've already told you. I'm going down with the gang to have a good time.'

'And what other reason is there?' Carson persisted.

'No other reason as far as I can think.' Bobby hesitated for a moment looking vaguely troubled. 'Now — er — just a minute, dad. There was another reason, but I just can't seem to remember — '

'So you can't remember?' Carson asked. 'Does it mean anything to you that you were going to tell your employer that you were going to Franton for the express purpose of seeing a possible client for the Stock and Share market?'

'No, it doesn't mean anything,' Bobby looked blank. 'Yet I have the oddest feeling at the back of my mind that it should. Look, what's going on here?' he asked sharply. 'What have you been doing to me? I feel as though some vital part has dropped right out of my life.'

'Some vital part has dropped right out of your life,' his father assured him. 'From hereon, my boy, you'll find that you are not only incapable of telling lies, but you are also incapable of remembering anything in connection with a lie. You see, that portion of your brain responsible for such acts has been completely neutralised. It just doesn't work. It's like a battery all connected but not charged up.'

'But this is ghastly,' Bobby protested, faltering. 'I can't seem to remember things properly, or what I am doing, or anything.'

'You can remember all the things you need to remember,' his father assured him. 'But matters connected with lies and deceit have dropped out of your knowledge.'

Bobby scratched the back of his neck

slowly. 'Well, thank heaven Betty Foster hasn't dropped out of my knowledge anyway, otherwise I might really have said a few things. I might even have been tempted to put my foot through that apparatus of yours. As it is — ' he stopped. 'Oh, I'm hanged if I know. I might as well go in to breakfast and see if that does anything towards restoring me to normality.'

'If by normality you mean the capacity to tell lies, breakfast will certainly not do it,' his father said. 'Nothing can. From hereon, my boy, you are going to lead a completely different life.'

2

The Fall Out

There could hardly have been a more dazed young man than Bobby Carson as he went to business that morning. All the way in the bus he thought of the extraordinary experiment, and wondered vaguely why he was experiencing no obvious after-effects. Yet, there it was. He felt as fit as he had ever done. His health, generally, seemed quite unimpaired. He had enjoyed a good breakfast, and by and large, everything in the garden was lovely.

The only troublesome point was this curious inability to link up certain events in his life. There were little gaps in it like a story with pages missing, and no matter how hard he tried he could not fit in the missing pieces. He was still pondering the matter when he reached the firm of Stock and Share Brokers where he was employed. He exchanged the usual confidences and quips with the rest of the office staff and then began his normal daily routine.

Some strange inner prompting during the morning finally led him to the private office of Jacob Henshaw, the managing director of the firm and typically a Stock and Share broker of the really tough tradition. Henshaw was a big man, massive shouldered, large stomached, and a specialist in highly expensive cigars. As usual the aroma of one of these cigars pervaded his office as Bobby knocked and then silently entered. The great man glanced up briefly, busy scribbling at his desk with a silver pencil.

'Well?' he grunted without looking up.

Bobby cleared his throat. 'There is just a little matter I would like to take up with you, sir,' he said politely.

'Well, what is it? Get it out, please, Carson. I am in a hurry. I have an important appointment.'

'It concerns your car, sir.'

Henshaw put down his pencil. He had bulgy, veiny eyes, with cheeks that hung far lower than they should have done.

'My car?' he repeated. 'What's the matter with it?'

'Nothing, sir, that I know of.'

'Then what the devil are you talking about?'

'It's like this, sir.' Bobby moved uncomfortably. 'I seem to have a vague recollection of having asked if I might borrow it this weekend — '

'Yes, you did,' Henshaw interrupted him brusquely. 'You said you had your eye on a possible client in Franton and wanted to borrow the car to give yourself the extra uplift necessary for the approach.'

'Oh, that was it.' Bobby looked relieved. 'Thank you for telling me, sir.'

'For telling you,' Henshaw repeated, staring. 'What the devil is the matter with you, man? Don't you remember what you said? The arrangements you made?'

'No,' Bobby replied miserably. 'That's just the point. I feel I should make it clear to you, sir, that the client is not available, therefore I shall not need the car as I'd expected.'

The great man's lips twitched a little round his cigar. 'As a matter of interest, my boy,' he said slowly, 'I rather object to your addressing me as though I were your chauffeur. I was loaning you the car for business reasons only, and I do not exactly like being brushed off with the remark: 'The car will not be required'. Why the devil,' the big man roared, 'don't you make more sure of your facts before you ask?'

'It's just that things have gone wrong since,' Bobby explained miserably.

'Oh, have they! Well in future, Carson, make sure what you're doing before you say anything or make a request. I shall now have to alter a lot of my own arrangements concerning that Rolls. I was going to have it brought out specially for you. Well, is there anything else on your mind? You looked damned miserable for you. Usually I find you the most cheerful person in the office.'

'Yes, sir.' Bobby shifted again with obvious uneasiness. 'It's as I said, sir, something has happened and I don't feel quite myself.'

'I see. Well, if that's all we'll say no more about it.'

41

Thankfully Bobby escaped. He admitted to himself as he did so that he had not the vaguest idea of what he had been talking about. Only the dimmest glimmering of remembrance had come into his mind as the great man had explained the reason for wanting the Rolls. All Bobby could remember about it was that he had asked for a car for some unknown dual purpose. Anyway that was now off his mind. The thing to do was to try to sort out if there were other untied ends lying about that needed to be put straight. Indeed the only shining light in his life at the moment was the fact that he could not by any mischance forget any detail of Betty Foster. She was the be-all and end-all of his existence outside the office. But oh, this infernal blank in his memory! It made him furious and bewildered by turns.

Somehow he got through the morning and then, as became his custom, he went to the Argos Café for lunch. It was here that he usually arranged to meet Betty Foster; her lunch hour coinciding with his. And sure enough, she was there as usual, wearing again the amazing hat of the previous evening.

She smiled brightly as she saw Bobby heading across the great expanse, dodging the waiters and the incoming customers. At last he gained the usual reserved table and settled down opposite her, his brow crinkled and his good-looking face a picture of melancholy.

'And what in the world is the matter with you?' Betty asked in surprise. 'I don't think in all the time I've known you that I've ever seen you look so utterly miserable.'

'Well, that may account for the fact that I *am* miserable,' Bobby replied. But before explaining he gave the order to the waiter and then continued: 'Something's happened to me, Betty, since last night. I don't know what, but you're not looking at the same chap with whom you danced yesterday evening.'

'Well the resemblance is uncanny even if I'm not,' Betty replied. Her grey eyes were wide and wondering, her heavily-painted mouth was pouting. Not that there was anything unusual in this; it nearly always was pouting. Just as though she was expecting a kiss and not getting it. Then, after a while she said: 'Maybe it's liver!'

'It's nothing of the kind.' Bobby looked indignant. 'I'm in perfect health, thank you. Physically, that is. What's wrong with me is mental.'

'Oh.' Betty still gazed at him in wonder. 'Well, does that mean that you can't smile or say hello or suggest something bright as you usually do? I can't make head or tail of you,' she confessed, 'and I must say that the change is certainly not for the better.'

Bobby did not answer her. He picked up his knife and fork and looked at them as though he wondered what they were, his thoughts obviously fathoms deep.

'What caused it?' Betty asked after a while. 'Something you ate perhaps?'

'No, an invention of my father's.' The words were out before Bobby realised it. He wondered himself why he had said it so promptly. It had just slipped off his tongue although he had made up his mind that he would not tell anyone about

44

his experience at his father's hands. Not that he saw any reason to suppress the information concerning the invention, but he did not know whether his father would wish him to speak publicly about it.

'An invention of your father's?' Betty repeated, then she looked rather vague. She knew well enough that Bobby's father was the great Dr. Carson, the celebrated 'Housewives' Choice', but this was the first time that she had ever heard his son refer to anything his father had invented.

'I cannot see,' she said, 'why an invention of your father's should make you look miserable. Is it something that he's done that is painful or what?'

'No, nothing painful. That's the odd part about it.'

'Then what is it?' Betty insisted. 'I can't sit here looking at you with your face as long as a fiddle without knowing the reason. At least tell me something. We are still friends, I suppose?'

'Oh, we'll always be that.' Bobby brightened for a moment and gripped her hand quickly. 'Betty, whatever happens to me, however strangely I behave, don't walk out on me. That's just one thing I couldn't stick, and heaven knows I've enough to put up with at the moment.'

'Is that meant to be a personal reflection on me or what?' Betty asked sharply.

'Nothing of the kind,' Bobby insisted. 'When I say I have a lot to put up with, I don't mean you. How could I?'

'Oh, well, all right then.' Betty smiled somewhat, but there was not much warmth in it, just the same. She was used to nothing but flattery from Bobby, and the sudden peculiar change in his methods of approach was a complete mystery to her. In any case she was not a brilliant girl, one quick to perceive the reasons for changes, so in this instance her only chance was to learn the truth from Bobby himself.

'You say it was something of your father's which made you miserable?' she repeated slowly. 'What, exactly?'

'It's a — ' Bobby stopped as the waiter returned and set the lunch down before them. When he had gone, Bobby resumed: 'It's an invention of my father's which affects the brain in some way or other and makes it that you can't do anything but speak the truth.'

Betty's eyes were wider than usual. 'Well, of all the peculiar ideas,' she said finally. 'I mean, who wants to speak the truth all the time? Get frightfully dull. It would be worse than being in Sunday School.'

'It's a far bigger subject than you'd imagine.' Bobby spoke with feeling. 'He tried it out on me chiefly because he considers or did consider that I'm the most consummate liar he has ever known.'

'Your own father said that?' Betty made a gesture of disgust. 'If my father said that to me I'm afraid I'd er — ' She stopped. She was going to say that she probably would have hit him, but she had remembered that her father was well over six feet in height and she was only five feet two, so the implication might have sounded ridiculous.

'Yes, this invention of my father's stops any tendency to lie,' Bobby explained. 'Certainly it's done it to me. I've discovered with the most horrible misgivings that I can't tell a lie even if I want.

47

I'm absolutely compelled to tell the truth.'

Betty's look was plainly incredulous

'It's true!' Bobby insisted. 'Just ask me some question. It doesn't matter what. I shall be compelled to give what I believe to be the truthful answer. Mind you, the answer I give is only the truth as far as I know it; it may not actually correspond to facts. What I mean is: if you were to ask me a scientific question, which would be most unlikely from you, Betty, I suppose I'd give you the answer to the best of my ability and let it go at that. It mightn't be the right answer. The point I'm trying to make is: I would not be lying.'

'The chances of me asking you a scientific question are as remote as flies at the North Pole,' Betty assured him. 'However, I will ask you one which I don't think you'll answer truthfully unless you wish to insult me. What do you think of my lipstick?'

Bobby looked surprised and then he studied her pouting lips. They were a brilliant pillar-box red, and seemed even bigger than they really were by reason of their flaring colour.

'Rotten!' he said frankly.

Betty dropped her fork. 'Rotten? But you never complained before. It's the same colour that I always use. It's Delamode Crimsonia, the very dearest and the very best.'

'It's still horrible,' Bobby said, frankly, picking up his knife and fork. 'If — if you'd like me to go further, I can say a thing or two about that hat of yours.'

'You already did last night.' There was a glint beginning to creep into Betty's eyes.

'Yes, but last night was before the invention had been at work. Now I can say frankly what I think of that hat. It reminds me of a cabbage with a blue hat-pin stuck through it.'

Most girls at this point would have flung down their knife and fork and left the café, never to return or seek Bobby's company again. But Betty had a deep liking for Bobby.

Yes, even now, in his most inexplicable mood. She was not sure whether she loved him or not — possibly she was too young even yet to know her own mind.

But she was fond of him and for this reason, in spite of the pasting he had just given her, she still remained seated, but she eyed him bleakly.

'Well, at least you've summed up my hat and my lips,' she said frankly. 'Is there anything else upon which you would like to give your views, Mr. Carson?'

'Plenty of things,' he agreed, setting about the chop with his knife and fork. 'That's just one trouble about being truthful, Betty. You very soon make yourself unpopular. I'm wondering how the rest of the gang are going to take it tonight, for whatever they ask me I shall be compelled to give them a truthful answer.'

Betty opened her mouth and then closed it again. She just did not know what to say. Finally she sought refuge in again tackling her lunch, and Bobby, too, made slow progress with the extremely tough chop. For a long time this wrestling match with the meat continued, both of them battling with somewhat blunt knives and leathery, half-burned food, and neither of them exchanging any more remarks. It was the arrival of the waiter again which finally broke the tension.

'Everything satisfactory, sir?' he asked smoothly, bending down from the heights over Bobby's shoulder.

'Anything but.' Bobby gave him a brief glance and tossed down his knife. 'Neither the young lady nor myself have ever tackled chops as hard as this. Surprises me that you don't hire out pick-axes in order to help the diners.'

'Really sir?' The waiter tried to look interested, but the glint in his eye was frigid. 'The service is precisely the same as it has been on other days, and I have not heard you register a complaint.'

'Other days were not the same as this one,' Bobby replied mysteriously. 'You can keep the rest of the menu, and my friend and I will go elsewhere in future.'

'Who says we will?' Betty demanded, staring. 'I like this café even if the food is a bit tough now and again.'

'It's more than tough,' Bobby said, getting to his feet. 'It's absolute granite, and I'm not going to put up with it.' He jerked his head briefly and because she usually did exactly as he suggested Betty got to her feet. She was beginning to look pink and embarrassed, but Bobby was not in the least moved. Stonily he surveyed the waiter.

'Check, please,' he asked curtly.

'Certainly, sir.' The waiter scribbled it out, and by a tremendous effort of will refrained from flinging it at his too-outspoken customer. Bobby took it, recovered his overcoat from the stand, paid the bill, then accompanied Betty to the outdoors.

'If this is telling the truth,' Betty said, 'I don't think much of it. Do you realise that I've had no sweet and I just don't like the taste of meat without a sweet to chase it away.'

'We're not going to encourage those blighters with that rotten sort of food,' Bobby told her. 'We'll find another café. Today we'll forsake the sweet. There just isn't time to find a fresh place to lunch. If it's all right with you, we'll meet again tonight, say outside the Williamson Memorial at half-past six. By that time I'll have thought of a fresh café to go to. How's that?'

'All right, if you say so.' Betty shrugged her shoulders. 'And I hope by that time you'll have recovered some sense. Please Bobby, don't get the idea that being outspoken is going to make me like you any the more. It isn't. In fact, it not only makes me dislike you but it makes everybody else dislike you as well.'

With that she went on her way back to the office, a very bewildered young woman. But her bewilderment was nothing compared to Bobby's. He detoured into a small park on his way back to the office, and cold though it was, he sat in one of the shelters trying to think things out. He had the feeling that the gaps in his life were less obvious now, that some sort of a pattern was forming, but most certainly this inability to say anything but the truth was frightening, and he hardly dared to think where it might land him.

That was the queer thing: where lying might have landed him had never presented the slightest worry, yet now he was going to tell the truth his worries were extreme. In fact it seemed to him that telling the truth was going to get him into far more hot water than telling lies.

So finally he returned to the office and performed his usual duties for the rest of the afternoon. During this period he had time to think, and decided finally that the Temple Café just outside the Strand would be the best place for a new rendezvous for the gang. The food, as he knew from one or two visits, was pretty good, and the service was fair. In general the place was the kind of establishment that was satisfactory in a general sort of way.

As usual he did not return home after office hours. He had a wash and brush-up and met Betty as arranged at six-thirty at the Williamson Memorial. He half-doubted if she would be there after the unusual happenings at lunch, but to his relief she was standing waiting, her coat collar turned up against the blustering wind.

'I forgot to mention something at lunch time,' he told her, when the preliminary greetings were over. 'And that was to tell the rest of the gang. They'll all be going to the Argos expecting us to be there.'

'No, they won't,' Betty said. 'They'll be meeting us here at any moment. I arranged for that on the phone. I gathered you must have forgotten it and it's going to be a long cold wait,' she added, glancing up and down the mainly deserted thoroughfare in which they were standing. 'Incidentally which café are we going to?'

'I thought the Temple Café off the Strand would be about the best. The service isn't too bad and the cuisine passable.'

'I see,' Betty said, hugging herself. 'Well, let's hope the others won't be long. I certainly want something to eat. I only got half a lunch, remember, thanks to you insisting on being truthful.'

'And I shall go on being truthful,' Bobby sighed, 'simply because it isn't in me to be otherwise.'

'You know,' Betty said, looking at him thoughtfully, 'if this happened to me I do believe I would bring an action. Yes, even against my own father. After all, there's a limit to the meddling that one's parents can do, and the mess it seems to have made of your character is unbelievable.'

'Well, it was all done with my permission,' Bobby replied. 'So even if I did decide to bring an action, which I couldn't being a minor, I certainly wouldn't have a leg to stand on. Oh, forget it! Maybe we'll get used to it later, or maybe I will.'

Betty looked very much as if she doubted this, but she did not argue the point for two members of the gang were just appearing in the far distance. Presently they caught up and it was obvious that they noticed the change in Bobby's expression from his usual good-humoured one.

'Anything the matter?' asked the taller of the two young men. 'You don't look particularly happy tonight, Bobby.'

'I'm not,' Bobby replied irritably, 'and don't waste time asking me why. Betty knows the reason and if she wants to explain — well, she can do. I'm getting about tired of it.'

The two youths looked at Betty questioningly but her round, full, red-painted lips were plainly set. If there was any explaining to be done, Bobby was going to do it. She was faithful enough to him not to give him away in any respect unless he himself wished it.

'It's just that Bobby got out of bed on the wrong side this morning,' she explained.

'Incidentally,' asked the shorter of the two youths, 'why are we meeting here in this blizzard-ridden spot? It's enough to give one pneumonia. What's wrong with the Argos Café all of a sudden?'

'Everything's wrong with it,' Bobby told them bluntly. 'Rotten food, poor service, exorbitant prices. I decided we'd change our rendezvous.'

'Oh you decided!' The taller one looked surprised.

'Any reason why I shouldn't?' Bobby asked. 'I've always been the leader of this little party, have I not?'

'All right, all right, don't get sore, I only made an observation. Since the Argos seems to be off the agenda, where do we finally settle?'

'The Temple Café,' Betty replied.

'That's all been fixed up and the sooner the others turn up the better.'

In another ten minutes the others had turned up, and beyond giving a brief statement that he did not approve of the service at the Argos Café, Bobby did not explain himself any further. Instead he led the way down the street, and in the space of fifteen minutes of cold, bleak walking the Temple Café was gained. Here Bobby wasted no time in making a permanent reservation for a table. This was easily fixed, and finally the party was seated and more than ready for a good meal.

When it was finally brought Bobby looked rather anxiously at the faces around him. He knew he could trust Betty, but he was not too sure of the others. The two girls perhaps — Joan and Elsie — were more or less to be relied upon, but the two young men were much more doubtful quantities. They were good comrades enough in the ordinary way of things, and prior to his father's extraordinary experiment, Bobby had liked them quite a lot. But he had never trusted them and now he trusted them even less. He only hoped they wouldn't ask him awkward questions, for he'd be compelled to say outright what he thought. This hope had hardly presented itself in his mind before a devastating question was hurled straight at him.

'What,' asked the taller youth, 'is the matter, Bobby? You're not the same fellow that we usually meet. We've become accustomed to seeing you grinning all over your face, supremely confident, talking your way out of any position in which you may find yourself. What has caused the change, anyway?'

'An invention of my father's.' The words were out before Bobby realised it.

'An invention of your father's?' the youth repeated blankly. 'And that's made you miserable?'

'It's a long story,' Betty interrupted, 'and one not worth recounting at the moment. For myself, I can hardly believe it but then, that's not surprising considering that Bobby here is such an expert on telling anything but the truth.'

'I was,' Bobby flashed back, 'but not any more. I've got to tell the truth now whether I like it or not.'

'What in the name of Satan are you rambling about?' the shorter youth demanded. 'First you say you've got to tell the truth, then you say it's got something to do with an invention of your father's.' He stopped, thinking. 'Let me see, now. Your father is a scientist, isn't he?'

'One of the best,' Bobby acknowledged.

'And you have to tell the truth because of an invention. That sounds suspiciously as though he's got some kind of lie detector. Is that it?'

'Well in a way,' Bobby admitted uncomfortably.

'Why tell them everything?' Betty asked. 'This invention of your father's is more or less a private affair, isn't it?'

'Not particularly,' Bobby replied, and wished he could stop answering so frightfully correctly all the questions asked him.

'Now let's get this straight,' said the shorter youth, leaning across the table intently. 'Is this invention that you speak of your father's something to do with making you tell the truth?'

'Yes,' Bobby agreed simply. He liked this particular youth least of all. The taller one was not a bad sort of fellow, but this shorter one always had a peculiar shifty look in his eyes as though he were always trying to learn something more than he should.

'In that case there might be something in it,' the shorter youth said.

'In it?' Bobby looked at him.

'Well, I mean an invention that can make one tell the truth whether you like it or not is something above the average. Come on and tell a pal,' he insisted. 'What exactly does this invention do?'

'You've already guessed it,' Bobby replied miserably. 'By some mysterious process which I think my father referred to as vibratory, it makes me tell the truth whether I like it or not, and a most harrowing experience it is. Betty here will tell you that my having spoken the truth to her was hardly flattering.'

'Hardly,' Betty agreed.

'Well suppose,' the shorter youth said, 'you tell me the truth about myself?'

'I wish you hadn't asked me to do that,' Bobby sighed, 'because I consider you the most shifty-eyed, peculiar sort of chap I have ever known. I don't regard you as a friend, merely as an acquaintance, and I'm not particularly sure that I regard even acquaintanceship as salubrious.'

'Well, of all the infernal — ' the shorter youth sat up sharply. 'I'm not taking that sort of talk from you, Bob Carson! You'll see! Come on Elsie, let's get out of this place. I don't know exactly what's happened to Bobby, but if you ask me he's nuts.'

Since the shorter youth and Elsie had decided to depart, the taller one and Joan did likewise. Not with such alacrity as the others, but they went just the same, leaving Bobby and Betty together finishing their meal.

'Well, that's that,' Betty said sighing. 'I wish you had not said that, you know. Jim is one who is liable to make trouble. He's a nasty piece of work at the best of times, and I hear, quite confidentially, that he has connections with quite a few unpleasant sort of characters.'

'I can't help it if he has,' Bobby gave a shrug. 'He asked for the truth and he got it.'

A sudden thought seemed to strike Betty. 'By the way what about Franton? Suppose we're going as arranged?'

'No,' Bobby shook his head. 'That's just what we're not doing. I told the boss this morning that I wouldn't need the car. Incidentally he was somewhat rude about the whole thing, but I had to tell him, hadn't I?'

'I can't think why.'

'Well, I mean, I was planning to go there purely on a pretext. The whole thing was based on lies, and after this experiment of my Dad's, I felt that I had to make things clear with my boss, so I did. He didn't like it, but at least I put things straight.'

'And you mean to tell me that our lovely weekend at Franton, with everything prepared and the hotel rooms ready, is wiped out just because you suddenly decided to become an angel?'

'No, nothing like that. We can still go if you like, in the ordinary way by train.'

'Not likely!' Betty sat back, folding her arms. 'The whole point of the thing was to go in style. I'm not going by train for anybody.'

'All right,' Bobby said. 'Then we don't go to Franton; that's all there is to it. As for the others, well, they don't matter anyway. It's perfectly obvious how they feel.'

As a matter of fact Jim Williams, the shorter youth whom Bobby had so liberally analysed, was positively fuming. When he and the taller youth and the two girls had reached the end of the street wherein the Temple Café lay, he came to a sudden stop, thinking. 'I don't see why Bobby should get away with this,' he said slowly. 'Do you realise what he's done? He's managed to get rid of all of us, but Betty's stayed beside him. I'd like to wager that the whole thing is a put-up job.'

'For what reason?' asked the other youth, puzzled. 'He's always done everything with us up to this point. Why should he suddenly change?'

'I don't know.'

It was clear that Jim Williams was doing a good deal of thinking. He was a crafty kind of youth, and he always liked to turn things if possible to his own advantage.

'On the other hand,' he said slowly, 'Bob may be telling the truth. After all, his father is a scientist, and I suppose an invention for making you speak the truth is possible. Does it occur to you, though,' he went on slowly, 'what an enormous advantage an invention like that would be to some people?'

The two girls and the other youth looked at him questioningly in the bright street lighting. They could not be expected to follow the machinations of his mind.

'What I mean,' he said slowly, 'is, that in the right hands — and by the right hands I don't mean a meddling old scientist like Dr. Carson is — this invention could be invaluable. I myself know quite a few people who would pay a heck of a lot of money for an invention like that.'

'Now just a minute,' Elsie said uneasily. 'I don't quite like the way you said that,

65

Jim. What have you got in mind?'

'Plenty,' he grinned, 'and I think the sooner I get it off my mind the better. Tell you what, you girls go with Joe here, and just leave me be for tonight. I've got some important business to attend to.'

'I don't see any reason why you should dash off like this, even if you have,' Joe objected. 'Which reminds me, we never asked Bob about the Franton business. We're not far off Saturday, it's time we got something arranged.'

'To hell with Franton,' Jim Williams said briefly. 'You can take it from me that Bob will never come round to that trip — he's got too much else on his mind. All right, I'll pay him out for the things he's said to me. You see if I don't! I'll get in touch with you later.'

He didn't give the others a chance to argue any further; swinging on his heel he walked swiftly down the street. He vanished round the corner. Elsie looked after him and sighed.

'This,' she said frankly, 'is absolutely crazy. I don't know who's the most barmy — Jim or Bobby Carson.'

Neither of the youths was barmy, and most certainly not Jim Williams. He had a very distinct idea in his mind and most of it was motivated by the desire for revenge for the way he had been spoken to. If there was one thing Jim Williams did not like, it was the truth about himself.

3

Theft

It was about an hour later when Jim Williams arrived in Harry's Pool Room in one of the more shoddy side streets of the city centre. He entered the smoky expanse and looked about him. After a while he spotted the man he was seeking. He went across to him as he stood beside the billiards table chalking his cue.

'Got a moment?' Jim Williams asked.

Nick Dawson turned in surprise. He was a particularly unlovely looking individual — square-faced, grey-eyed, with a broken nose which spoke of days past in the ring.

'Well, if it isn't Jim Williams!' he exclaimed in surprise. 'Haven't seen you around for many a month, my lad. Where have you been keeping yourself? In high society?'

'You might call it that.' Jim jerked his

head. 'Come over here, Nick, will you. I've got something that might interest you. The game can wait.'

Nick Dawson looked rather reluctantly at the billiards table then with a sigh he put down his cue and lumbered after the youth across the poolroom. They settled down at a corner table and Jim jerked his head quickly.

When the drinks had arrived he said slowly: 'How would you like an invention, Nick, which would make it possible for you to force anybody to tell the truth?'

'Eh?' The ex-pugilist stared blankly. It was perfectly obvious that he was not a brilliant man, and this suggestion was about the most incredible one he had ever heard.

'An invention to make people tell the truth?' he repeated hazily. 'What the hell sort of a thing would that be?'

'Just listen carefully,' Jim Williams said slowly. 'Did you ever hear of Dr. Carson?'

'Er — let me think now.' The pugilist scratched his chin. 'Dr. Carson? Yes, I seem to remember something about him. Don't they call him 'Housewives' Choice' or something? He puts out all those cute gadgets — patent tin-openers and bottle stoppers and all that kind of thing?'

'That's the man,' Jim Williams gave a quick nod. 'Well, he's the one who has made an invention that can force you to tell the truth whether you like it or not.'

'Oh, a sort of a lie detector, you mean?'

'No. Something much more complicated than that and much more thorough. You see, I happen to know his son. These past few weeks I've been one of his closest friends. Tonight there's been a bit of a blow up all because of his old man's invention.'

And in detail Jim Williams gave all the facts. The pugilist sat listening, drinking his beer at intervals and getting his rather slow-moving brain to work to try to grasp the possibilities.

'I can't see an invention like that being of much use to me personally,' he said frankly, 'but probably the boss might be pretty interested. Supposing I put it to him?'

'Just as you like.' Jim Williams shrugged. 'The point is this. I believe I can fix it so that you can get this invention. I don't mean just plans or specifications but the actual thing itself. It'll cost a good deal of money, but for five thousand I can probably swing it.'

'Five thousand quid!' Nick Dawson repeated astonished 'Where the hell do you think I could get that kind of money?'

'I don't care where you get it or how, but possibly the boss that you speak of may be more willing than you are and may be willing to pay for the invention. I can't think why he shouldn't. I'm not a criminal like you are.'

'Who's a criminal?' Nick Dawson interrupted, glaring. 'And keep your trap shut down here. I don't want that kind of talk getting about.'

'Sorry,' Jim Williams grinned. 'But between you and me you're not exactly lily white are you? There aren't many things you haven't dabbled in, bar murder, perhaps.'

'All right. So I make a living by my wits,' Nick Dawson admitted. 'Why shouldn't I? The boss pays well for it.'

'That's one reason why he should be

the one to be interested. You tell him all about it and see what he says. But remember, five thousand quid is the price I demand before I do a stroke.'

Jim Williams knew exactly what he was about. This was not any haphazard visit that he had made, in the hopes that he might be able to cash in on Dr. Carson's invention. It was a carefully thought out plan. Jim knew very well that Nick Dawson was a smalltime thief with probably a bit of blackmail on the side; there were plenty of unsavoury deals in which he had been mixed up. That he was not the brains behind those criminal activities was well known. Evidently the brains belonged to the boss and Jim Williams was reasonably sure that a man of intelligence would definitely see the possibilities of a machine that could force anybody to tell the truth.

'How long do you suppose it will be before you can get an answer?' Jim Williams asked. 'I don't feel inclined to wait and hang around and hope for the best; there are plenty of others who would be interested in this apart from your boss.'

Nick Dawson got to his feet clumsily. 'Maybe I can even settle it now,' he said. 'The boss is in his office at this moment.' With that he went shambling away across the poolroom. Jim Williams sat back, glanced at his beer, left it untouched and waited. He had never been quite sure whether the boss was on the premises or not. Now he knew the facts. Evidently the boss was also the proprietor of this distinctly unsavoury poolroom.

Fifteen minutes passed before Nick Dawson reappeared. He came across to where Jim Williams was still seated at the table, his beer flat and still untouched. For surprisingly enough Jim Williams was no drinker. He merely ordered it to be in the swim.

'Well?' Jim asked, glancing up. 'What luck?'

'I'm not quite sure. The boss doesn't seem to be able to make head or tail of the way I tell it. Maybe you'd better see him yourself. Go into him, will you?'

Jim rose and went across the little office

at the back of the poolroom. Once within, he closed the door behind him and stood looking at the sleek, well-dressed man seated at the desk by the window. It was littered with correspondence, bundles of notes, small piles of silver currency, and all the odds and ends of a man used to handling a poolroom. He himself was probably tall when standing. Dark-haired, good-looking after a fashion, but with a certain steel-trap tightness about the mouth that gave the clue to his real nature.

'Sit down, son,' he invited cheerfully.

Jim Williams flushed. If there was one thing that infuriated him it was to be called 'son' when he imagined himself to be such a powerful man of the world. Nonetheless he did sit down.

'Now!' The boss sat back in his chair. 'What's all this rigmarole that Nick was trying to tell me? Something about a gadget that makes you tell the truth?'

'It's not a gadget,' Jim Williams said curtly, 'it's a scientific invention and I've seen what it can do. It's ruined about the best friend I've ever had, though come to

74

think of it I don't know whether he really ever was a friend or not. Anyway the fact remains he does nothing now but tell the truth, where only yesterday he was about the biggest liar ever.'

'And you think a machine has done it?'

'I don't think it has, I know it has. He told me so himself. And since he has not been able to tell a lie, I took it as being the truth.'

The boss sat back and reflected. It was clear he still did not quite understand what the whole business was about, but he was quite willing to learn.

'Nick Dawson mentioned something about Dr. Carson,' he said presently. 'Am I to understand he is the inventor of this so-called truth gadget?'

'That's right,' Jim Williams acknowledged. 'The friend I've just told you about is Bobby Carson, Dr. Carson's son. As far as I can make out, it looks as though the old man experimented on his son, and the result was so good that Bobby is in the unfortunate position that he cannot tell a lie, even if he wants to.'

'And what prompted you to come and

tell that broken-nosed henchman of mine all about it?'

'Simply that I felt that he might know the best contact. An invention like that is far too useful to be left in the hands of a scientist. The possibilities would be wasted. Why, in your hands, or in the hands of any man in your position, I should imagine that an instrument like that would be invaluable.'

'Yes, very probably.' The boss's expression did not give anything away. 'Am I to understand that Dr. Carson performed with this apparatus at his own home?'

Jim Williams considered. 'Well, I should imagine that that would be the case. Yes. In fact I'm almost sure,' he added, thinking. 'He wouldn't do a thing like that publicly. Bobby hasn't said that it all happened at home, but I think I can rely upon it that it did.'

'In that case then, am I to understand that Dr. Carson has a laboratory in his home or some sort of electrical workshop or something like that?'

'Definitely he has. I've seen it.'

'Very interesting.' The boss gave a

broad smile that showed white teeth. 'Well, thanks for the information, son, I'll think it over.'

Jim Williams started. 'You'll think it over? But I'm not prepared to wait while you think it over. If you're not interested I know plenty of others who will be — '

'I did not say I was not interested,' the boss interrupted. 'I said that I wanted to think it over. I can't suddenly decide what I want to do with an invention like that. You just hang around; I'll let you know.'

'You mean tonight?'

'Not necessarily. Tell you what you do!' The boss leaned forward over his desk. 'I'll tell Nick Dawson what my final decision is. Just keep dropping in. He'll let you know soon enough.'

Jim Williams got to his feet. He didn't quite know where he stood, but it was obvious that the boss didn't intend to commit himself any further, for he had already turned back to his normal office business. He gave a brief nod of farewell, and at that Jim Williams went out of the office and stood outside the closed door, irritated and wondering. He could not be quite sure but it seemed to him that he had been given what is technically known as the brush-off.

The boss himself made no further moves for half an hour then, when upon enquiry he learned that Jim Williams had left the poolroom, he turned to the telephone and lifted it from its cradle.

'That you, Arthur?' he asked quickly. 'Come over will you. I think we have something interesting.' There was some kind of non-committal grunt from the other end of the wire and the boss replaced the phone on the cradle.

Some ten minutes later a short, strongly-built man came into the office.

'Well, boss, what is it?' he asked.

'Sit down.' The boss nodded to a chair. 'I think we've happened on to about the most useful thing that ever was. And, by the grace of Providence, it's a young sucker of about eighteen who's given me the information. The most astonishing part of all is, I believe he even has a price for this information. But I can tell you what he can do with that.'

The wide boy known as Arthur grinned

and sat down, waiting for the next.

'It seems,' the boss said, 'that a scientist by the name of Dr. Carson has invented some kind of a gimmick which makes one incapable of telling lies. Now do I have to explain in detail how useful that could be, especially in our profession?'

'It sounds very much to me like a lie detector,' Arthur decided flatly, 'and I'm having nothing to do with an instrument like that.'

'I don't think a lie detector has anything to do with it. That is purely a device which operates electrically from the nervous jolt a body gives under the influence of guilt.' The boss seemed vaguely proud of his scientific knowledge. 'No, this is something very different. It makes you tell the truth. And there's absolute evidence of it in that Dr. Carson's son is the first victim, or patient, or whatever you call it. From what I gather from this youngster, young Carson was quite a liar until today. And now he only tells the truth. Now it seems to me,' the boss continued, musing, 'that if we could get our hands on an invention like that there's no limit to what we could do.'

Arthur did not comment immediately, because he was not sure upon whom it was intended to use the Lie Destroyer. He, himself, had quite a few things that he liked to keep in the dark, and if this instrument went to work on him — !

'I'm not so sure, boss,' he said slowly, 'that I want anything to do with it. It might be dangerous. Anyway, how does the thing work?'

'At the moment I haven't the least idea, but I daresay we can find out, even if we have to force Dr. Carson himself to tell us.'

'Mightn't that be rather dangerous? He's a pretty important man.'

'I'm perfectly aware of that,' the boss replied curtly. 'What I'm thinking of is his son. If that young man is unable to tell a lie and we can corner him there is every possibility that he will tell us all we want to know. Personally, I think that's a marvellous idea,' the boss continued, rubbing his hands. 'The very fact that the son can't tell a lie will be the one means by which the father's invention can be stolen.'

'Yes, it's cunning all right,' Arthur agreed, still uncomfortable. 'But even if we've got such an invention, what's the good of it? I mean, we know amongst our own lot that none of us tell the truth as a matter of principle; where would be the point of making us start revealing everything?'

'I wasn't thinking of our own crowd; I was thinking of far bigger game. You know the whole basis of blackmail,' the boss continued, 'is to keep quiet about somebody's guilty secret. Now in many cases guilty secrets are not revealed, but with the operation of an instrument like this practically anybody could be forced to tell secrets that they believe are forever hidden. There are tremendous possibilities. At the moment I am only just grasping at the very fringe.'

It was at this point that Arthur became more amenable. It suddenly dawned upon his obtuse mind that he would probably be perfectly safe from the instrument, and for that matter the rest of his comrades as well. It was those outside the unholy circle who would be affected.

'And what about this lad who's given you the tip?' he asked. 'If you just brush him off and don't do a thing he might get nasty. It might get us into a good deal of difficulty.'

'Yes, I thought of that,' the boss admitted. 'I understand from Nick Dawson that this lad's price is five thousand pounds. He won't get that, or anything like it, but I will give him enough to keep quiet and give me certain information. Chiefly concerning Dr. Carson's son and his movements. Once I know those there's a good deal I can do and that's where you come into it.'

'Okay. Any time,' Arthur agreed. 'But it seems to me that if we are to be on the safe side we ought to call a scientist into this. Since a scientist invented this truth gadget it will take a scientist to understand it. If we run the thing wrong, heaven knows what will happen.'

'Once we get the gadget I'll have Dr. Findon see what he can do,' the boss said. 'He's helped us out on other occasions. Do you remember that business where he told us to use thermite to destroy that safe which we couldn't open?'

'Yes. He's just the man.'

'However, the first thing to do is to get hold of this gadget. That means that the first move also is to find this boy again, who has the impudence to think that he can get five thousand pounds. You leave this to me, Arthur, and stand by for fresh instructions.'

For Bobby Carson, quite unaware how far things had gone since he had told Jim Williams the truth about himself, the days that followed were dreary ones indeed. To him life was a complete humdrum monotony, without the constant indefinable thrill of being able to lie about any situation. It meant that he had to live like an ordinary person, do an ordinary day's work and live like a 'good little Eric' all the time. It was infuriating. He began to wonder if it might not precipitate a nervous breakdown.

It was even more infuriating when he noticed his father's complacent smile. It was as though he had accomplished a masterpiece. He was quite unconcerned with the fact that his son had lost his so-called friends, lost all interest in life and very nearly lost Betty too. At the last moment, however, she had relented somewhat and still remained loyal to him — despite the fact that he was anything but the youth that she had formerly adored. All the sparkle had gone out of him and that, to Betty, was the deplorable thing. After a week of his lie-free existence Bobby was seriously considering whether or not he ought to enter a monastery or something equally drastic. The future definitely seemed as though it did not hold anything of interest.

'The next thing that will happen to me will be that I shall lose my job,' he confided to Betty about a week after the experiment had been tried out on him. 'You just think. I'm in the Stock and Share Broking business, and there could not be anything worse in that line than not to be able to tell a lie. I can see the look in the boss's eye that he's considering what to do about me, next. And I can't say I blame him.'

'Funny, isn't it,' Betty said, thinking, 'how unpalatable a thing the truth can be.

Yet, you know, in some ways I envy you. It makes you absolutely honest whether you like it or not. I rather wish I were that way myself, sometimes.'

'You needn't,' Bobby told her sourly. 'There is nothing more exasperating than to have to give the truth about everything, no matter what it may be.'

At the moment they were seated at their reserved table in the Temple Café. It was a quarter-past six in the evening and though they had each other's company, they both had the memory of faces that had apparently gone forever. For not since that evening a week ago had Joan and Elsie and the two boys presented themselves. It was clear that they had walked out for good. Evidently the idea of one of their number speaking nothing but the truth, and that one their leader into the bargain, had proved too much for them.

'Not that it really matters, I suppose,' Betty said, as this line of thought pursued her. 'They weren't much use to us, only it did make for more company. The point I want to get at is: what are we going to do?

We keep coming here, going around together, trying to get used to the idea of you never telling a lie, and that seems to be the sum total. Frankly, Bobby, it is getting monotonous.'

'Well, what do you want to do?' Bobby gave her a frank look. 'I suppose you would like to walk out too, and join the great big world where nothing but untruths are spoken from morning till night?'

'I did not say that,' Betty looked hurt. 'I merely said that we ought to do something — about ourselves, I mean. Get married for instance,' she said with a sudden plunge.

'Well, I suppose that is possible,' Bobby agreed, 'but the way things are looking in my line of business I think we ought to postpone it. It isn't safe. If I lose my job just after we got married, what then?'

'I'd take a gamble. Look at it this way,' Betty went on seriously. 'I've a great regard for you, Bobby, and I feel that if I walked out, you wouldn't have a friend left in the world, except perhaps your mother. What I mean is: you must have somebody beside you. You're not a normal person. A person who goes around never telling a lie really needs a keeper or something like that.'

Bobby grinned faintly. 'You know something, Betty, I wouldn't feel half so badly about this if there were others in the same boat as myself. I think it's the fact that I'm alone in my glory that's getting me down. I've been seriously considering whether I ought not to ask Dad to put his invention on the market. Then of course, hundreds might use it and I should no longer be a phenomenon.'

'Then why don't you ask him?' Betty asked, spreading her hands.

'I don't know why. I get the impression somehow that he would not take kindly to the idea. At the moment he's just content to gloat over the fact that he's stopped me lying. I really believe the scientific achievement he has made — for it definitely is a scientific achievement — is the main thing that interests him. The financial possibilities don't seem to have occurred to him, but they have to me. If I could only get him to trade the invention or something like that — ' Bobby lost himself in moody speculation.

When he spoke again he seemed to have abandoned the subject as too complicated, for he didn't refer to it any further. It was fifteen minutes later when he and Betty left the café having in mind the intention to visit a cinema. Their intention, however, underwent an abrupt change, for on leaving the café they suddenly found that two men who had evidently been hanging about the doorway, closed in behind them. A voice spoke briefly, kept low, but nonetheless audible.

'You see that car straight in front of you, you two? Get into it and ask no questions.' Bobby half-turned, but the voice added: 'You don't need to look now; it might be dangerous. Just do as you're told. You — and the girl. Quick!'

Bobby, had he been alone, would probably have stopped to argue. Not so Betty. She gave one brief, wide-eyed, panic-stricken glance over her shoulder, then darted straight for the big black saloon that was standing at the kerb. Bobby followed her, settling in the upholstery. The door slammed as one of the men, tall, broad-shouldered, a soft hat pulled well down over his eyes, came and looked at them briefly through the window. Then he climbed in beside the driver and uttered a brief word of command:

'On your way, Arthur, and make it quick!'

The short, stockily-built Arthur did not waste a moment in hurtling the saloon away from the kerb. Within a few minutes he was out of the side street wherein the café lay and moving quickly into the main traffic stream that went through the centre of the city. Everything had happened so rapidly that Bobby and Betty hardly realised what was transpiring. They looked at each other then finally Bobby leaned over the front seat, addressing the bigger man.

'What's the idea of this, anyway?' he demanded, 'or don't you know that it is criminal to abduct people in this fashion?'

'This is not abduction,' the big man answered briefly. 'It's just a little matter of business. In case you don't know it, young man, you've suddenly become very important.'

'Well, I'm glad to hear it,' Bobby sighed. 'Funny you should say that; I was just considering going into a monastery.'

'You were what?' The big man looked over his shoulder in blank amazement. 'Into a monastery?'

'Never mind,' Bobby sighed, sinking back into the upholstery. 'It's too involved to explain. In fact, you're the one who should do the explaining. What's the idea of this? Stop this confounded car!'

'With pleasure, later on,' the big man chuckled. 'For the moment, just sit tight. You're neither of you coming to any harm, are you?'

'Not yet,' Betty said nervously. 'Depends what you have in mind.'

'It is not what I have in mind,' the bigger man replied. 'It's what the boss decides. I'm purely acting on orders. Can't blame a man for doing that.'

He said no more than this so Betty and Bobby were left to conjecture what the whole business was about. Deep down, Bobby had a pretty good idea what was at the root of everything, but for the time being he held his council. There was just a chance that he might be wrong.

The car carried on swiftly through the main city traffic, branched left, then followed a mainly quiet route after which it twisted and twined so much, in and out of side streets and crescents, that neither Bobby nor Betty had the vaguest idea where they were heading. Certainly, when the car finally pulled up outside the shoddy façade of an obviously cheap gaming saloon, they had not the least conception of how they had managed to get here. The big man and the one called Arthur alighted to the pavement, and the rear door of the car was flung open.

'Outside!' said the bigger man briefly, jerking his thumb.

Betty alighted first. Bobby followed her. Together, looking and feeling very much like naughty school children, they entered the wide open doors of the poolroom then paused for a moment, overpowered by the haze of tobacco smoke in the place and the general stifling atmosphere. To Betty it was a complete shock. Bobby, a little more experienced in these matters, endeavoured to look at home, but deep down he was beginning to feel very much afraid.

'Keep going,' the big man said, coming up in the rear. 'Straight across the poolroom here. See that door over there by the wall? That's it.'

There was no alternative. Bobby moved forward reluctantly, Betty beside him. Together they threaded their way amongst the habitués of this smoke-clogged den. Finally they reached the door, knocked upon it, and entered.

The big man watched them though he did not keep close to them. The man within the office was a totally different proposition. Well dressed, handsome, with a dry smile which revealed the intense whiteness of his teeth.

' 'Evening,' he said politely, rising, and he produced a chair for Betty. Bobby, he merely looked at, and made no attempt to make him comfortable.

'Naturally you're wondering who I am?'

'All I know is: that if you're guilty of

abducting my friend and I there's going to be trouble,' Bobby said flatly. 'In case you don't know it, my father is Dr. Carson, a very eminent scientist, and he'll certainly make things hot for you and those two thugs outside who did the job for you.'

'I am already aware, my boy, that your father is Dr. Carson.' The proprietor of the saloon sat down slowly. 'And it is for that precise reason that you are here. It was quite by chance that your lady friend happened to be swept up as well. But that was just in the way of things. It may even prove to be an advantage.'

'Advantage!' Betty started. 'In what way? What on earth can you want with me?'

'I'm not sure yet.' The boss gave her a malignant glance, then he looked back again at Bobby as he half-perched on the edge of the table. 'It's you, my boy, I'm interested in. I understand that you are one of those remarkable people who find it impossible to tell a lie.'

'Correct,' Bobby snapped. Then he gave a start. 'But who on Earth told you?'

'Never mind. It just happens to be my business to get to know things. Your father has invented a Lie Destroyer, hasn't he?'

'What if he has?' Bobby asked brusquely.

'Don't answer a question with a question, my lad, or it will be the worse for you. Has he or has he not?'

Bobby did not reply. There was one advantage when he felt impelled to tell the truth; he now found that he had enough control to be able to keep silent. Which was one way round his difficulty, anyway. Plainly it was a way that did not please the proprietor. His steel-trap mouth tightened and the gleam came back into his eyes. 'I asked you a question,' he said slowly.

'I heard,' Bobby answered, but did not add any more. But suddenly he recoiled from the desk and indeed nearly fell on the floor before a savage slap right across the face.

'That,' the boss said, looming over him, 'is just to show you that I am not here to play games, young man. Did your father invent the Lie Destroyer or didn't he?'

'Yes, he did,' Bobby answered sullenly.

'And he tried it out on you?'

'Yes.'

'With the result that you now find it impossible to tell a lie?'

'Yes,' Bobby said for the third time, and gave Betty a bewildered glance.

'Thank you,' the boss said cheerfully, rubbing his hands. 'That's all I wanted to know.'

He settled down again at his desk and meditated for a moment or two.

'I don't see how you know all this?' Bobby blurted out. 'Somebody must have told you. It could only have been one of those rotten pals of mine. Jim Williams I'll wager! Just about the kind of shifty thing he would do.'

'How I come to have the information is really of no concern,' the boss said, still meditating. 'The main point of interest is that this Lie Destroyer intrigues me immensely. So much so that I have decided to use it myself.'

'If you want a tip from somebody who's undergone the misery of having the power of lying destroyed, you'll have nothing to do with it,' Bobby said seriously. 'And anyway you are about the last type of man on Earth that I can imagine wanting to lose the power of telling untruths.'

'That,' the boss said, 'is not very funny. I don't want it for my own personal use as a victim, I mean. I have other reasons for requiring it. It seems to me that your father, in keeping it to himself, is doing the world a great disservice.'

Bobby glanced around him, saw a chair and drew it up. This time he sat down without being asked. It was just beginning to dawn on him what this was all about, and it struck him as singularly peculiar that it might prove the answer to his own wishes. Namely, that he be not alone in glory.

'I had you picked up for a definite reason,' the boss resumed. 'I have a proposition to put to you, young man. I'm willing to pay you the sum of five thousand pounds, if in return you see to it that I get that invention of your father's together with all details as to how it works.'

'Five thousand pounds,' Bobby repeated

blankly. 'That's a fairly large sum for the type of man I judge you.'

'Never mind what type of man I am. How does the proposition appeal to you? I happen to know that you're the kind of young man who likes money, and that before this — er — unfortunate eradication of untruthfulness from your mentality you spent quite a deal in different ways. But you managed it then by your extraordinary ability to lie. Now that you cannot lie, that particular source of finance is cut off, so I imagine that five thousand pounds would be welcome.'

'I never heard of anything quite so outrageous!' Betty burst out. 'Not only have you the effrontery to abduct us but you even ask Bobby to sell his father's secrets to you! The thing's absolutely impossible! First thing you know, we'll have the police on your track for this.'

'Quiet, Betty,' Bobby gave her a warning glance. 'Let me handle this — '

He looked again at the boss. 'Let me get this absolutely straight. For five thousand pounds you want my father's instrument complete. Is that it?'

'That,' the boss concurred, 'is it. A perfectly straightforward business proposition.'

'And suppose I were to do this, what guarantee have I got that you will tip up the money?'

'None, I'm afraid. All I can do is give you my word. I will pay up because you could make things very awkward for me if I didn't.'

Bobby relaxed into silence, rubbing a finger thoughtfully along his top lip. The boss watched him intently. Betty looked from one to the other, half-started to speak, then changed her mind.

'I have to admit,' Bobby said after a while, 'that the proposition appeals to me. Not exactly the five thousand pounds — though that is certainly an incentive — but the fact that the Lie Destroyer can be made general property. I would, of course, have to arrange it so that my father would not know that I was responsible for the disappearance of the machine, because under those circumstances it would amount to theft. For that matter, I can't quite see why you are willing to pay me five thousand pounds when, with a little ingenuity, you can steal the equipment for yourself.'

'Maybe because I'm an honest man,' the boss grinned.

'Bobby!' Betty exclaimed horrified, 'you're surely not going to entertain this proposition? It just isn't to be thought of.'

'Isn't it?' Bobby gave her a grim glance. 'You're not in the same position that I am, Betty; you don't know how much dad has hurt me and how willing I am to get my own back, if it comes to that. He had no right to perform such an experiment, even though I agreed to it.'

'That sounds to me very much like sense,' the boss said cheerfully, delighted to discover that the whole business was running so smoothly. 'Am I to understand that you agree to my idea, then?'

'Why not?' Bobby asked after a brief pause. 'That invention has been lying around ever since dad experimented on me. He seems to have completely forgotten all about it. Having achieved his objective with me, he doesn't do anything more. I don't see letting five thousand pounds slide by under my nose that easily. If I remove the machine he'll probably never notice that I've done so.'

'It's in his laboratory then?' the boss asked casually.

'Certainly it is. Pushed away on a shelf like any old radio set. In fact, that's what it looks like.'

'I see.' The boss looked thoughtful. 'And how does it work? Do you happen to know that?'

'I know a little.' Bobby hesitated. 'Something to do with vibrations, as far as I know. I'm not a scientist, though. Only dad himself could explain that.'

'Yes, or another scientist,' the boss suggested.

'Well, that's up to you. If you want the machine, I'm willing to try and get it, but before I hand it over I must see that five thousand pounds in cash. None of your cheques, please.'

'Fair enough!' The boss smiled, spreading his hands. 'I find you quite a good businessman, Mr. Carson. I think we can leave it at that, then. When you have that machine, notify me here. The address is:

The Acme Poolroom, Anderson Street, East Central, and I will remark that if either of you mention your visit here tonight or tell of this proposition to anybody else it might prove a little — er — shall we say awkward for you, later on.'

'I'll say a good deal,' Betty said indignantly, jumping to her feet. 'I've every right to resent being whisked off into a car against my will and then to sit and listen to this appalling proposition.'

'You strike me as a sensible young lady,' the boss remarked, looking at her levelly. 'If you are not, I'm sure that Mr. Carson here will endeavour to correct your viewpoint.'

'Don't worry about her,' Bobby said. 'I'll very soon straighten things out in that direction. Very well, Mr. — er — ' he hesitated.

'The name is Andrews. Cliff Andrews, and thank you for being so sensible.'

Which seemed to be the top and bottom of the interview. The two were free to go, which they did. The moment the door had closed Andrews pressed the intercom.

After a moment or two Arthur came in, expectantly.

'Get anything out of them, boss?' he enquired.

'All that was necessary.' Andrews briefly related the interview.

'But that's crazy,' Arthur objected. 'You've found out where everything is and then you go and offer that young sucker five thousand pounds to get you the invention. Why, I could get it myself in five minutes, and never mind paying anybody.'

'That, my enterprising friend, is just what you are going to do, believe me. I only offered young Carson five thousand pounds to sort of oil the works. He told me all I wanted to know. The instrument is in the laboratory at his home, that it's on a shelf, that it looks like a radio set. I imagine even mugs like you could hardly fail to locate it.'

Arthur scratched his head, completely dead to the insults.

'I don't get it, boss,' he said frankly. 'What's going to happen when the apparatus disappears? The boy'll start talking and say we've stolen it.'

Andrews chuckled. 'He'll have to prove that, though, won't he? Just listen here a moment.' He crossed the office and opened a cupboard. From within he took a recording apparatus and set it on the table. Without commenting he switched on the rewind button and watched the tape whirling back to its original starting point. Arthur had seen this apparatus at work before, but had never particularly concerned himself with the mechanics thereof.

'The whole thing is perfectly simple,' the boss said, when the tape had come back to its starting point. 'I recorded the entire conversation with that boy. You'll notice that the microphone is on top of the deed cabinet there. Whether it was noticed or not I don't know. But there was nothing to show that it was alive, since the recorder was hidden in the cupboard there. Now the point is this — if that invention is stolen — as it will be — the first thing young Carson will say is that we have stolen it. Or that I have. If the police question me I shall play over the recording of the interview I had with Carson wherein he is willing to accept five thousand pounds to remove the instrument himself.'

'Then what?'

'I shall deny ever having received such an apparatus, though of course I shall freely admit that I made an offer for it. The blame, thereby, will be switched back to young Carson and he will have to explain where the set has gone.'

'Will he find that so very difficult?' Arthur asked scratching the end of his thick nose. 'I mean, if he's supposed not to be able to tell a lie, his father will believe everything he says, and he'll say that we did it.'

'Ah, yes! But he cannot *prove* it,' Andrews insisted. 'That is the point. In other words it is simply a classic example, my friend, of passing the buck. We know where the thing is. Now we'll get it. Whatever trouble there is this recording will take care of. Needless to relate the recording ceases where the interview ends.'

There was no doubt that the scheme was decidedly cunning in so far that

Andrews had found out all he wished to know and at the same time switched the blame to the quite innocent Bobby. There was nothing left now except for the thick-necked Arthur to put his own plans into operation. And that night he did so. Indeed he went to work before Bobby had returned home, for the simple reason that he and Betty turned into a cinema and there stayed until nearly eleven.

In that time Arthur had done all he needed to do. Long skilled in the art of burglary it was not a very difficult problem for him to enter the quiet annexe at the rear of the big Carson home. Carson himself was not working in the laboratory that night. A public announcement in the paper had showed that he was lecturing upon the dangers of atomic power, which meant that he could not possibly be home until towards midnight; and of course, his wife was certainly not in the laboratory. In fact she was in the lounge watching the television, so Arthur had a perfectly easy task. To locate the apparatus was simple, and in a matter of ten minutes he had come and gone.

4

Confession

Bobby, entirely unaware of what had happened during the evening whilst he had been with Betty, spent a greater part of the night sleeplessly wondering whether he had done the right thing in promising to sell his father's invention. Part of the time he slept: the rest of the time he debated ways and means. Could he perhaps contrive some method whereby it would look as if burglars had broken in? In short, could he make the business look convincing enough to shift the blame from himself?

All the mental gymnastics that he performed were torn up by the roots the following morning, when, to his amazement, he learnt that the invention had disappeared.

It seemed that his father had not been so disinterested in the Lie Destroyer as he

— Bobby — had thought. Apparently he had been in the habit of studying it almost every day, usually early in the morning. Working out fresh details and adding new modifications to a sketch plan, leaving the machine itself upon its shelf until such time as it would be needed. And now it was gone with nothing to show how.

'Well, I just don't understand it,' Bobby's mother said frankly. 'Nobody came last night, that I do know, unless it was during the early hours of the morning when we were all in bed.'

'Well, obviously it was,' Carson said irritably. 'It couldn't have been any other time. The fact remains, it's gone. The only thing that I can do is call the police. That invention is extremely valuable. In the wrong hands I shudder to think what could happen.'

Such was the conversation that took place over the breakfast table. Bobby himself made no comment. He sat listening in wonder then in rising anger as it dawned upon him that he had been cheated out of the five thousand pounds upon which he had banked.

'Definitely it must be thieves,' he said abruptly.

His father glanced at him. 'I should have thought, Bobby, that that was more than obvious. Your mother has made the same observation. If only I could have something to work on!'

'There is just the possibility,' Bobby said slowly, 'that I may know who the thieves are.'

'Oh?' His father's eyebrows rose. 'That's extremely interesting. Well, who are they?'

'I'm thinking about Jim Williams,' Bobby added. 'He used to be one of my friends. That was in the days before I lost the power of lying. I know that some of the things I said to him made him extremely vindictive. Now Jim Williams is a big friend of several doubtful characters who hang out in the East End.'

'Oh, come to the point,' his father interrupted impatiently. 'What's all this got to do with my vanished apparatus?'

'Just this,' Bobby plodded on stolidly. 'I wonder if some of these precious pals of his have put two and two together concerning your invention, dad, and made a grab at it? It wouldn't surprise me in the least.'

Carson looked rather shaken. It had never occurred to him that there could be such a violent repercussion from his experiment upon his son. That making him incapable of telling a lie had resulted in the machine being stolen was something that had never entered into his calculations. He cleared his throat a little to hide something of the confusion that he felt.

'The police can deal with this,' he decided flatly. 'Immediately after breakfast I'll call them.'

'Before you do that,' Bobby said slowly, 'why not give me a chance to see if my hunch is right? I know the kind of characters with whom Jim Williams frequented. I may be able to discover something.'

There was a certain look in his father's eye that Bobby did not like.

'I have the feeling, Bobby,' Carson said, deliberately, 'that you know a great deal more about this matter than you're telling. Perhaps the fact that you're incapable of telling a lie may prove extremely useful on this occasion. I'm going to ask you an outright question. Do you know who has taken that apparatus of mine?'

'Yes,' Bobby replied miserably, and cursed himself for being unable to say otherwise.

'Well, whom?' There was a steely glint in Carson's eye.

'To the best of my knowledge, it's a man called Cliff Andrews.' And Bobby went into the whole story of the previous evening. Attacked relentlessly by his father and cross-examined as thoroughly as though be were in court, he was compelled to admit the whole miserable business of the five thousand pounds proposition.

'Why,' Mrs. Carson exclaimed; horrified, 'the whole thing is unbelievable! You were willing to sell your father's invention, Bobby! I just can't credit it!'

'Why not?' Bobby flashed back. 'It's all very well for you two to sit in judgment upon me. You just don't know what I'm going through or what I shall have to continue to go through. You ought to know, dad, scientifically, that if you stop one particular outlet of Nature that she'll take revenge by using another outlet. The fact that you have stopped my tendency towards untruthfulness has made me unusually vicious. In fact, I hate everything that you have ever done, and particularly that invention which you have used on me. I don't for one moment regret that the invention was stolen — and even less do I regret that I agreed to steal it for the sum of five thousand pounds. The only thing that does annoy me is that it has gone without my getting the five thousand pounds.'

Carson did not utter a word. He went on with his breakfast in complete silence. Bobby wondered why. He had expected a torrent of abuse, and the fact that he did not get it was somehow more disturbing than the actual thing itself.

The moment breakfast was over Carson wasted no more time. He left the house and some half-hour later he arrived at

Cliff Andrews' Poolroom to find that the illustrious Andrews was not present. There were, however, one or two waiters swabbing the floors and cleaning the tables. They looked up in surprise as the short, angry-faced scientist entered. Within a few minutes he had been told that Andrews was never there before evening, but it took him nearly another quarter of an hour to discover where he could locate him at his private address. Consequently Carson at last tracked down the elusive pool saloon owner in a quite comfortable flat in a fashionable part of the city.

Carson wasted no time in coming to the point, but by the time he left the apartment he was reasonably sure that all the aces were in Andrew's hands.

Bobby for his part, spent a most uncomfortable day at the office, hardly daring to think what was going to happen to him later. He lunched with Betty as usual and gave her the full details. There was nothing she could do but come to the same conclusion as himself — namely that Cliff Andrews must be responsible for the robbery. So for once, Bobby did not delay when he left the office. By arrangement with Betty he cancelled his usual meeting with her and returned home to discover the lay of the land.

He found his father grim and austere, and obviously only controlling his temper with extreme difficulty.

'Well?' Bobby asked awkwardly, after he had come into the lounge and given his mother an affectionate hug across the shoulders. 'Was I right, dad? Was Cliff Andrews responsible for the theft of your invention?'

'He doesn't admit as much, but there is not the least doubt in my mind that he is,' Carson answered, his face grim. 'He told me a very long story, most of which bears out what you told me. Namely, that you were willing to accept five thousand pounds to sell me out.'

'Not to sell you out,' Bobby insisted. 'To get my own back on that invention. Please keep it in its proper perspective, dad.'

'In many ways,' Carson said slowly, musing, 'I feel that I am responsible for this lamentable state of affairs, therefore I am not going to pitch wholeheartedly into you, Bobby. The fact remains that Andrews, whether he be responsible for the theft or not, holds the whip hand, chiefly because he has a complete sound recording of your interview with him last night.'

'He has what?' Bobby gasped, alarmed.

'Word for word,' Carson confirmed. 'He played it to me while I was there. Which, if it were used in any court of law — though I am in some doubt as to whether the law accepts a sound recording as evidence — would leave no doubt but that you are the guilty party. Since that is the case there is nothing more I can do in the matter. This man Andrews is a clever psychologist. He knows that on the one hand, that I cannot prove that he stole the apparatus; and on the other hand he knows that I will not go to court and indict my own son. No father worth his salt would do that, no matter how grievous the loss. The only thing that would make him do it would be incontestable proof, and that I have not got.'

'But you can't mean that you're going to let him get away with it!' Bobby exclaimed. 'Why, heaven knows what he will do with the invention.'

'Perhaps you should have thought of that when you made your bargain,' his father said sourly. 'It didn't seem to worry you very much then what Andrews might do with it. No, the only thing I can do is let it go — I shall not call in the police, because, as I say, the proof is so fragile it just wouldn't hold up. The only thing I can do is build a fresh instrument, and when and if my original apparatus does turn up in the public eye, I shall bring an action. Unfortunately, the instrument is not patented. I was intending to patent it when all the modifications were complete. But at the time of the theft they were not complete. The action I shall bring will be for theft of the original invention because I do hold the original sketches, which might be enough to swing the balance in my favour.'

There was silence for a moment.

It was Mrs. Carson who summed up the situation clearly.

115

'In other words, it's all as good as lost,' she sighed. 'I should imagine that this man Andrews will be up to all the dodges when he does decide to bring the apparatus out.'

'I'm afraid so,' Carson admitted moodily. 'The one other hope is, that now they have got the instrument, these men will not understand how to use it.'

'I wouldn't be too sanguine about that,' Bobby put in quickly. 'Andrews said something about getting a scientist to work the instrument out. You probably heard that in the recording.'

'Oh, yes.' Dr. Carson seemed to remember. 'I believe I did. But believe me no ordinary scientist will be able to solve how that instrument works. One fraction out and it might cause the most irreparable damage to the poor devil upon whom its power is used. No. I'm afraid there is nothing I can do but make another machine. Of course,' Carson continued, reflecting, 'there is another side to this matter. I don't see that the instrument, no matter who uses it, can do anything but bring good. There cannot be a better purpose than to destroy the tendency to lie in human beings, now, can there?'

Bobby gave his father a rather sad look. Inwardly he was astonished that a man of his father's immense scientific capabilities could be so innocent in assessing the criminal possibilities of his machine.

'I can think of lots of unpleasant uses to which that apparatus could be put, Dad,' he said quietly, 'but for the sake of your peace of mind — and my own for that matter — I'll refrain from mentioning them. I'm quite sure that Andrews didn't steal the machine so that he could start a crusade for better living amongst the masses.'

Carson's only response to this was a glance of disapproval, then he shambled out of the lounge, with the obvious intention of going to the laboratory to start work on the construction of a new Lie Destroyer.

Bobby looked across at his mother.

'How do you feel about all this, Mum?' he asked.

'My main reaction to it, Bobby, is that

your father should never have started the thing in the first place. I warned him at the time that it could bring nothing but trouble. It is no use him singling you out as a scapegoat just because you were willing to sell him out. I do believe I should have done the same thing in your place. The point is: he should never have dabbled. Leave well alone. As for your tendency to untruthfulness, I do believe you would have outgrown it in time.'

'Thanks.' Bobby gave a rather rueful smile. 'On the strength of that I think it's about time I had something to eat. I didn't stay at the café this time, so where is it?'

His mother smiled and got to her feet.

And at about this time Dr. Findon, Cliff Andrews's specialist scientist who had helped the saloonkeeper in so many dubious schemes in the past, was just rising from an intimate study of the Lie Destroyer. Findon was a clever scientist with quite a few imposing degrees behind his name. But certain unethical conduct had ruled him out of the normal spheres of the profession and he had descended

118

more to the level of criminal consultant. In other words, whenever one of the lower grade needed scientific advice, whether it be for the cracking of a strong room or the scientific murder of an unwanted person, Dr. Findon could usually be relied upon to provide the answer. He was a tall, thin-faced man, tight-lipped, who had a habit of speaking in the most analytical terms. Few had ever seen him smile — perhaps because he had no good reason to do so.

'This,' he said, tapping the long lean forefinger on top of the Lie Destroyer, 'is quite the simplest and yet the most brilliant electronic invention I have ever come across.'

'The point is,' Cliff Andrews said, 'does it work?'

'I cannot think of any reason why it should not,' Findon answered, looking at it again. 'It incorporates the principle of electronics and emits a wavelength which, as far as I can tell at this cursory examination, should be responsible for deadening certain cells, especially in the brain. To sum it up, I imagine that Carson achieves his objective by deadening certain areas behind the subconscious or he may even neutralise these areas completely, thereby making the person under treatment incapable of telling a lie.'

Andrews rubbed the back of his neck. He was a far better saloonkeeper than he was a scientist.

'All I want to know,' he said deliberately, also tapping the top of the apparatus, 'is, can this be used to force anybody, man or woman, no matter how obdurate they might be in will-power, to tell their deepest secrets?'

'Again, no reason why not,' Findon replied. 'The only possible way to find out is to experiment. But before you do that I must go more carefully into an analysis of anatomy. My knowledge of the brain is not what it might be. Not that I don't understand the human brain — at one time I was an expert — but I have drifted into other fields, notably physics, so I must revise a lot of my knowledge before I pass an opinion. What I would suggest you do is: keep this apparatus safely under lock and key until I have examined the whole business more thoroughly.'

'I'll do that all right,' Andrews prom-
ised. 'Nobody's going to get their hands
on this machine if I know it. There was
far too much difficulty in getting it — not
in actually having it stolen — I mean in
the repercussions afterwards. Anyway,
doc, thanks very much. As soon as you
have the full dope let me know — '

5

Tide of Blackmail

Dr. Findon wasted no time on his analysis. In fact, for two days and nights he worked almost consistently, rubbing up his not inconsiderable knowledge of surgery and neuroscience, but also in checking up all the points he had located concerning the apparatus itself. Two days later he reappeared again in Cliff Andrews's Poolroom.

'Well?' Andrews asked, as the scientist came into his private office. 'Have you got it all worked out?'

'I have gone a darned sight further than that,' the scientist answered quickly. 'I have not only solved what this machine does, but I have also discovered that Dr. Carson has been remarkably limited in dealing with the possibilities of this machine.'

'Oh,' Andrews raised his eyebrows,

'that sounds interesting. Take a seat, doc, and tell me all about it.'

Findon settled himself and lighted a cigarette. He was looking somewhat harassed after his continuous labours, but just the same behind the harassment there was the gleam of triumph in his eyes.

'You're not a scientific man. Andrews,' he said, after a moment or two, with some bitterness, 'so what I am about to tell you may go over your head — but anyway, here it is. What Dr. Carson has done is devise an electronic vibration that neutralises that portion of the brain responsible for the conduct of personal behaviour. Do you understand that?'

'Yes,' Andrews said dryly. 'I think I'm capable of understanding that much.'

'Good. Now try and understand this. That vibration has been devised by Carson so that he can needle-sharp focus it upon the particular area of the brain concerned. I suppose by that means he has to do as much wangling as a photographer when he's trying to get his camera into place. But you know, that's where he's absolutely slipped up, much to my astonishment. There is no real need to go through all that palaver. The fact of the matter is that this vibration can be sent out anywhere, anyhow, indiscriminately as it were, and it would only affect the portion of the brain responsible for behaviour. What I mean is: if it were produced on a giant scale, sent flowing outwards like radio waves from a radio station, it wouldn't cause any other part of the brain to be affected. Only that one special area. Understand?'

'Just about, yes. What you mean is that Carson wasted time in focussing, pin-pointing and arranging. There's no need for it. It couldn't have affected any other part of the brain anyhow.'

'That is it, exactly,' Findon agreed with satisfaction. 'Therefore the possibilities are enormously widened.'

He leaned forward intently in his chair.

'Consider this,' he said earnestly. 'If we were to build an apparatus like this, on a very big scale, so that it generated this vibration with enough power to affect everybody within a twenty-mile radius from its source, we would find that everybody within that twenty-mile radius had suddenly become truthful. The whole thing's simple. What is astonishing to me is that Carson hasn't thought of it. Or if he has he hasn't had time to get round to it. It means,' Findon continued, 'that we have a weapon of colossal power that nobody will be able to stand against. They won't know where it's coming from nor why they suddenly become truthful. All we have to do is to build enough of these instruments all patterned on the design of this original one, and before long we can have the whole country telling the truth.'

'You're sure of that?' Andrews asked slowly.

'I'm convinced of it. I haven't spent the last forty-eight hours wading through all the facts not to be sure of them.'

'All right! All right! Don't get touchy. It's just that it's such a huge proposition that I can't take it in.'

'If you like to hand the scientific side over to me, I'll see that the whole thing's done and completed as rapidly as possible,' Findon added. 'I warn you though, that it's going to cost many thousands of pounds to build machines like this, and also remember that they must be done secretly. Divide the thing up over several firms, then one can't tell the other what they're doing. No one person will know anything. Do you understand?'

Andrews was lost in thought for a moment.

'Why it means that wherever we take one of these instruments people will simply say exactly what they think, what they're doing, what they're aiming at. Think of what a politician would do when he suddenly finds that he's got to tell the truth, or a criminal, or anybody,' Findon added dryly. 'All of us are more or less scared of having to tell the truth 'cos if we do we're bound to reveal something that we've kept hidden. It looks to me that with machines like this we can start the biggest blackmail racket that ever was.'

The truth of the matter was that Dr. Findon was a far cleverer scientist than Dr. Carson — or if not cleverer he had more imagination. He never accepted any scientific instrument or theory at its face value. He always wanted to see how it would look when it was developed to the full. By this means he had arrived at his present conclusions concerning the Lie Destroyer. As he had said there was no earthly reason why the vibration, tuned only to that one particular portion of the brain, should not be disseminated in one continuous out-flowing wave.

The effect would be much the same as a radio wave. A radio wave can only materialise through the particular setting of the condenser on the receiver. It cannot affect any other portion of the receiver. In the same way this vibration would not be able to affect any other portion of a brain. By such a means most of England, in fact all humanity, could be at the mercy of these mysterious machines which would force truthfulness whether it was desired or not.

'This,' Andrews said, slowly rubbing his hands again, 'is about the greatest thing that has ever happened to us, Findon. Yes, by all means take over the scientific side. I shall have enough to do in other directions. Planning whom we are going to attack specifically. I'm not interested in the mass of the people — the silly little secrets of the average man and woman are not worth bothering about.

'What I want is something big, some big man or woman, who'll be willing to pay and pay heavily to keep such a thing quiet. It all has to be organised and arranged into one perfect military operation, if you like to call it that. Anyway, go to it, and as far as money is concerned the sky's the limit.'

Findon nodded and got to his feet. A few moments later he left the office to set his plans in motion. Which, had the average man and woman of Britain known it, was a sinister compaign against them. The days went by and Dr. Carson kept a constant watch on the media for some mention of his apparatus having come to light, but nothing was revealed. He said nothing but he went on working steadily in his laboratory apparently upon a duplicate of the original Lie Destroyer.

Bobby seeing him now and again got the impression that the new Lie Destroyer was of an entirely different design to its prototype. It looked less like a radio set and had a great many new gadgets attached to it, together with a new internal wiring. The only conclusion that he could come to was that his father was putting in the various modifications that he had designed for the other set, which had so abruptly vanished from his possession.

Andrews, however, was no fool. Though he appreciated the value of giant machines, he also knew the power of small ones, whereby single individuals could be tackled and forced if need be to reveal some of their deepest confidences.

The first man to fall before one of the smaller machines was Simon Caldecot. For many years he had been a self-styled philanthropist, giving away thousands to this or that charity, and generally setting himself up as one of the most beneficent of human beings. Andrews had long suspected that the genial Caldecot was not so frightfully generous as he appeared. One evening he paid him a visit, along with Arthur, and under the impression that he was to be shown a new electrical machine from which he might make a reasonable profit, Caldecot did not argue when the two men plugged the apparatus in and stood it on the desk. The only thing he did notice was that they stood behind it, whilst he was seated in front of it.

The outcome of the interview was brief, and very much to the point. Caldecot, like Bobby Carson, lost the power of lying, and under the impact of direct questioning, was forced to reveal that most of his fortune had been made through what would be called in ordinary circles, bare-faced robbery. He gave every detail, even while he wondered why he did so. In the end he found Cliff Andrews grinning at him cynically over the apparatus.

'Very interesting,' the saloon owner said briefly. 'Would you like me to print all that information, Mr. Caldecot? Or would you prefer to make a donation to keep it hushed up?'

'I don't understand this!' Caldecot banged his fist on the desk. 'Why the devil did I tell you all that? There's no reason why I should. Dammit, Andrews, I've known you for years but I never thought you were a hypnotist — if that is the explanation?'

'No it isn't the explanation.' Andrews chuckled and gave Arthur a glance. 'The real explanation is one which I prefer to leave you to guess at. The fact remains, Caldecot, that you've suddenly become a truthful man, which you should be as a philanthropist, of course.'

'That electrical machine has something to do with it,' Caldecot said, staring at it.

'Correct.' Andrews jerked his head to Arthur for the instrument to be moved away and unplugged. 'The fact remains, Mr. Caldecot, that for the sum of one hundred thousand pounds you can have peace of mind. I shall not say a word. If on the other hand, you prefer to be obstinate, then of course the papers are likely to have a very juicy story about the great philanthropist.'

Simon Caldecot paid his one hundred thousand pounds. He was too bewildered and too scared to do anything else. And it was only the first of many. Andrews in his position knew quite a number of so-called public figures, renowned for their 'blameless' lives. But they didn't stay blameless very long, under the relentless impact of the Lie Destroyer, and Andrews' carefully planned questions.

Money began to flow towards Andrews in an ever-increasing river. In fact he was almost having more fun with individual attacks on public figures than in hearing from Dr. Findon that the giant machines were not far from being completed. From the small individual onslaughts were rich rewards, and Andrews was a happy man.

There was only one shadow that stalked his life, and that was the fear that one day he might accidentally stand in front of the machine instead of behind it, and thereby lose the one thing which he valued — his power to lie his way out of a difficult situation. However, such a predicament had not yet arisen and he hoped devoutly that it never would.

Nevertheless this matter of standing behind the vibratory projector when it was in use led him to question Dr. Findon about it.

'How is it,' he asked, 'that I can stand behind the machine and have complete immunity, and yet the machines on a giant scale will affect everything within a twenty-mile radius? Within a twenty-mile radius means, I assume, a complete circle, as in the case of a radio station where the waves flow out in circles from the radio aerials?'

'The bigger machines will incorporate a different arrangement,' Findon explained. 'The small projectors simply transmit the vibrations frontwards through that queer-looking lens. The big ones will have lenses all round them and will emit the radiation in every direction. As you say, within twenty miles. The machine itself being at the centre of the circle.'

'But that's crazy. We'll come under the influence as well.'

Findon smiled acidly. 'Not the way I have it worked out, we won't. Those operating the machines will be within a heavily insulated cabinet. Remember that to achieve their effect the machine has only to be on for about a minute, or even less. Once they have sent forth their vibrations, the job is done. They can then be switched off and moved to another point of vantage. Anyhow the insulated cabinet — I call it that for the sake of convenience — will save the technicians themselves from getting involved in the vibrations. Believe me, I haven't left anything to chance. The last thing I want is to be forced to tell the truth, and I'm perfectly sure that is your wish also.'

Dr. Findon was too valuable a man for Andrews to make a curt retort, so he kept quiet. In any case his own particular problem was answered, and he knew that as far as the small projectors were concerned he would always be safe as long as he stood behind them.

So the racket went on. Famous men and women found themselves mysteriously assailed at intervals. Sometimes they actually saw the projector, as had been the case of Simon Caldecot, but others never knew what really happened since Andrews operated it from outside the home or office of the particular individual concerned.

Many were the ingenious methods that

he had to use, always helped by the bull-necked Arthur, and sometimes even the projector had to be powered by batteries carried around in Andrews's private car. But no matter how complicated the situation he always got his way. And so effective was the instrument that those who fell beneath its power were compelled pretty much to do as Andrews asked or else risk public exposure. There was here, definitely, the nucleus of one of the biggest rackets of all time.

It was inevitable as these happenings increased, that news of them got to the ears of the Press, and Dr. Carson, naturally, was one of the many thousands who read of them. 'There's no doubt but that my Lie Destroyer is behind these happenings,' he told his wife. 'The more I think about it, the more I think I shall go and visit Scotland Yard. Probably they might be able to handle the situation. If they can I've still got my original sketches to prove that the Lie Destroyer is really mine.'

'You're quite sure,' Ethel asked anxiously, 'that that won't involve you, Mark?'

'How can it?' he asked brusquely. 'I'm not trying to blackmail people and get information from them. It's this man Andrews. At least I suppose it is. Naturally the papers don't say who's responsible. They daren't.'

Bobby, seated at the other side of the breakfast table, didn't make any comment. It seemed to him that everything he had predicted had come true. And now his father was forced to realize that not everybody viewed the Lie Destroyer as a means to reform humanity.

'How's the new instrument coming on, Dad?' he asked. 'Making any progress?'

'Yes. Satisfactory enough,' his father replied. But somehow his manner seemed evasive. 'There are a lot of things I want to incorporate into it, which were not in the original machine.'

'Oh!' Bobby looked surprised. 'It struck me as being efficient enough, anyway.'

'Basically, yes.' Carson pondered for a moment or two. 'But there were a great many things I left out, which I shall certainly not do this time. And I shall also take care that nobody steals this one.

Anyhow, to get back to the point. I'm going to see the police and see if they can do anything about it before the whole business gets out of hand.'

Carson kept his word. That morning he went to Scotland Yard and after a good deal of preliminary moving from one department to another he finally found himself in the office of Chief Inspector Houghton.

Houghton was a thick-shouldered, florid, and probably, very unimaginative man. He made Carson comfortable enough, for Carson was famous, but how much he believed the story of a Lie Destroyer, was very doubtful.

'I can only repeat that everything that I have told you is perfectly true,' Carson insisted. 'Surely the one thing you want to do is to break this blackmail racket that seems to be seizing the city. Dammit, man, there's evidence of it everywhere. Politicians, actors, actresses, financiers, famous people in every walk of life indeed. They're simply at the mercy of this thing.'

'But it's all so unbelievable,' Houghton

protested. 'I mean, a machine that can make you tell the truth, even granting there is such an instrument. I don't wish that to be a reflection on you, Dr. Carson, but I can't quite see how it operates in such a manner as to make blackmail possible.'

'Perfectly simple,' Carson said brusquely. 'Imagine that you have some very deep secret that you don't wish anyone to know about.'

'Well?' Houghton looked vaguely uncomfortable.

'Well, if this instrument were tuned on you, and you were asked point blank if you have a particular secret that you don't want to tell, your answer would immediately be, yes! And if you were cross-questioned again, immediately afterwards, you'd find you were telling that secret before you realised it. You see, the initial impact of the machine is so tremendous that it leaves the victim somewhat stunned — I mean incapable of maintaining a discreet silence. After a time, it does become possible to control the emotions sufficiently not to blurt out an immediate answer. But just at

138

the beginning, even those with the strongest mentality are incapable of holding themselves back.'

'I see. Rather like the enemy has the initiative.' Houghton laughed rather heavily.

'If you like,' Carson's glance was cold. 'Anyway, inspector, that is the situation. I suggest that you look into it right away and question this man Andrews. Otherwise this racket is going to grow, and if it gets into really big proportions it will probably undermine our entire social structure.'

Houghton nodded. He probably did not wish to look obtuse, but he certainly did. With some misgivings Carson went on his way again hoping that the man of the law would get a result. Be it said to Houghton's credit he did immediately set to work on the business, and during the morning he visited Cliff Andrews's saloon.

As usual, Andrews was not there, but the waiters knew better than to play games with a Scotland Yard inspector, so gave Andrews's private address.

Shortly before noon the inspector

presented himself. Andrews was at home and he made himself as cordial as possible, but certainly he did not guess the reason for the inspector's visit. He imagined that some infraction of the law in regard to the saloon was the cause for this interview.

'I am here, Mr. Andrews, on a rather peculiar mission,' the inspector explained, more uncomfortable than he had ever been in his life before. Chiefly because he was not at all sure what he was driving at.

'Oh, I see,' Andrews motioned to a chair. 'Do take a seat, inspector.'

Houghton did so, and as he went back to his own chair beside the desk, Andrews depressed a foot button that rang in the next room. In there was Arthur. He had been in the midst of a conversation with Andrews when the inspector had arrived, so as usual had made himself scarce. Also in that room, was a recorder. Andrews never left anything to chance. He had thousands of reels of recording tape, which covered practically every interview he had had in his office or at home. And this occasion was no exception. A signal was sufficient for Arthur to set the apparatus in action. Also in that room was the smaller version of the Lie Destroyer, standing on its tripod looking very inoffensive.

Arthur waited. Then presently he crossed to the wall, moved a switch, and a tiny peephole came into view. He looked through into the main room where Andrews and the inspector were deep in conversation. All Arthur had to do was to wait for a double buzz on the bell, which would mean that the Lie Destroyer must be put into action. Obviously upon the caller and not upon Andrews.

Indeed Andrews had already lured many unsuspecting victims to his home for the particular purpose of using the Lie Destroyer upon them. He had only used this method when he had failed by every other means to deal with the situation.

'I believe, Mr. Andrews,' Houghton said, coming straight to the point, 'that you are the possessor of a scientific instrument which makes lying impossible?'

Andrews casually inspected his fingernails and pressed twice upon the button with his foot.

'Am I?' he asked, raising his eyes.

'The Yard,' Houghton continued, 'is very much interested in these blackmailing activities which are going on at present. Never mind how I got my information. Answer my questions if you will.'

'I have no need to answer your questions and I'm not going to,' Andrews replied levelly. 'I'm too old a hand for you to try to scare me, inspector, if that is what you're trying to do. And you should know better than to ask a man a question like that without proof.'

'I have all the proof I need,' Houghton lied. 'The invention of this Lie Destroyer was originally Dr. Carson's. It was stolen from him and he has given me quite enough facts to satisfy me that you are responsible for the theft.'

'A very dangerous observation,' Andrews commented, sitting back in his chair again. 'You should have more sense than make it.'

'At the moment I'm talking unofficially,' Houghton snapped. 'As man to man.'

'Oh, I see.' Andrews gave a wide grin.

'On the strength of which you expect me to admit everything. Is that it? You should know me better than that.'

'What I'm trying to do,' Houghton explained, 'is to give you a chance to come out into the open. If you don't wish to, then I shall have to use other means to make you. You have a Lie Destroyer. It was invented by Dr. Carson and you stole it. Either give me some facts or I shall have to put the whole machinery of the law to work, and that means that you'll get run in, and quickly. In fact I've been waiting for a chance like this for some years, Andrews. I never have liked the way you've handled things for a long time, but you've always managed to stay on the right side of the fence.'

'And not being entirely crazy I shall continue to stay on the right side.' Andrews gave a casual glance towards the adjoining room. In that one glance he saw all he needed. In one corner of the fanlight there was a tiny red lamp showing. Nobody, unless they knew what to look for would have noticed it — but to Andrews it meant that the Lie Destroyer had been in action for the required length of time for it to become effective. And Arthur, who was now skilled in the use of the machine, had no doubt taken good care that it had affected only the inspector and not his boss.

'Tell me something, inspector,' Andrews said after a moment. 'Have you any secrets?'

Houghton gave a start. This was the exact opening that Carson had warned him about when the Lie Destroyer was at work. Hardly thinking what he said he answered: 'Yes, quite a few, why?'

'I'd like to hear some of them.' Andrews waited.

'The secret which I think is the biggest skeleton in my cupboard,' Houghton said slowly, speaking in a far away voice, 'is the uncompleted case of Henry Armstrong.'

'Yes, I remember him,' Andrews acknowledged. 'He was a child murderer whom nobody ever managed to find, wasn't he, or something? I remember the case a few years back.'

'I was on that case,' Houghton continued. 'I actually had my hands on the man, and then I let him go.'

'Very strange conduct for an officer of the law, inspector. Why did you let him go?'

Andrews never took his eyes from the inspector's face. This was not a matter of hypnotism; this was shock tactics. Very shortly, within perhaps thirty minutes, the inspector would have recovered sufficiently from the impact of the instrument to control his words and his thoughts. At the moment he was like a man mesmerised. He simply spoke freely and without giving a single thought to his choice of words or statements.

'About that time,' Houghton continued, 'I was in pretty desperate financial straits. I would have done anything to get some money. And here I had a chance. Henry Armstrong offered me fifty thousand pounds to let him escape. Now, as a man of the law I should have ignored that bribe, for of course, it is the most dangerous thing you can do to try and bribe a police officer. But I accepted it. Don't ask me what came over me at that time — I simply knew that I must have some money. Everything depended on it.

The circumstances don't matter now. Anyway, I was given the money, and Henry Armstrong was gone while my back was turned. That was what happened.'

'For your information,' Andrews said, smiling cynically, 'that has been taken down on my tape recorder. Would you like me to play that back to Scotland Yard? I think the Assistant Commissioner would just love to hear it.'

Houghton put finger and thumb to his eyes. He was just beginning to realize just how much he had said, though even so there was a deep confusion in his mind, just as there had been in the case of Bobby when he had been slowly coming out of the mist of the instrument.

'Before you start accusing me of stealing Lie Destroyers, and telling me what the law is going to do, think over carefully what you have just told me. Because if you don't, that recording is going to the Assistant Commissioner, and I'd advise any other inspectors or men of the law who think they have just cause to attack me, to keep quiet. Is that understood?'

'Why on earth did I ever say all that?' Houghton asked. 'I just don't understand it. What happened anyway?'

'Plenty.' Andrews motioned towards the door. 'Get out, inspector. You're making the air smell bad.'

Houghton went, taking his skeleton with him. Just how far the interview had affected him was shown in the papers that evening. The heading read:

YARD INSPECTOR COMMITS SUICIDE

Dr. Carson, when he read the column, compressed his lips. It could only mean that the Lie Destroyer had worked so fast on Houghton that he had not been able to recover himself, and obviously haunted by the fear that Andrews would expose him, he had put an end to things. And this was only the beginning.

At least it taught Carson a lesson. He did not again visit Scotland Yard because he felt that in doing so he might lead other inspectors to destruction. That was the last thing he wanted. Deep down he was amazed at the sinister possibilities of his invention. It had never occurred to him when making the apparatus to correct Bobby's tendency for lying that such a desperate situation could arise. For desperate it was.

After the death of Chief Inspector Houghton, the blackmailing racket went on. Scotland Yard looked into it of their own accord without any prompting from Carson, but nobody seemed to get anywhere. Certainly there were no more reports of suicides among Scotland Yard Inspectors but the fact remained they did not make any progress. Carson knew why.

In every instance each man investigating had some kind of secret he wished to keep to himself and the apparatus ruthlessly uprooted it and made it that it was an absolute case of discretion being the better part of valour. So Andrews went on unchallenged.

Bobby during this time was finding life a little less irksome. Secretly he was interested in the happenings with the Lie Destroyer. He searched the papers assiduously and listened to all the radio and television bulletins, exchanging notes with

148

Betty. He did not feel so alone now. Others were in the same condition as himself, and there is nothing more uplifting when feeling miserable to find that somebody else is miserable as well.

By this time Betty had more or less grown used to Bobby's eccentricity, as she politely called it. She was ready for his outspokenness, and by degrees she was even adapting herself to liking it. More than once she privately conjectured whether or not she too would like to have the Lie Destroyer used upon her. Not because she was not altogether an honest young woman, but because she felt it would put her more in sympathy with Bobby if she were in the same condition as himself.

Meanwhile events were moving behind the scenes as far as Andrews was concerned. He used a great deal of his hush-money in acquiring suitable sites up and down the country for the installation of the large-sized projectors. Nor was he alone in this endeavour. He worked constantly in cooperation with Dr. Findon, who weighed up the scientific possibilities of the sites chosen, proximity to power lines, or failing that to a river where power could be generated by this means; and there was also a small army of 'trusted' men under the direct supervision of the bull-necked Arthur. Altogether an unholy gang was at work in different parts of Britain, making preparations for the biggest onslaught of truthfulness ever known.

In certain cases the police questioned the matter, but like their contemporaries at Scotland Yard they got nowhere. Either Andrews lied himself out of his predicament, or else he unearthed some secret which made mouths suddenly become tightly shut.

It was early in the New Year that the first three giant projectors were put into action, and as Dr. Findon had estimated, they functioned over an area of roughly twenty miles. The machines were situated in the north, the midlands, and just outside London. The sites where they were normally housed were disguised as factories manufacturing candyfloss and sweetmeats.

When in operation the machines were taken in a van labelled 'Apex Candyfloss' and thereby moved to whatever point of vantage was required, the power of the instruments either coming from a hook-up to the normal power line overhead, or else from a massive battery system devised by Findon himself.

By this method the projectors were as mobile as the detectors used by the police in tracing television sets, and on the 9th of January all three projectors went into action in different parts of the country, disseminating their vibrations in an ever-widening circle over an area of twenty miles in the three sectors of Britain.

It was now no longer a case of individual blackmail that Andrews was aiming at. Indeed the whole scheme was not entirely his own. He was partly working on Findon's ideas also, and this embittered gentleman, thrown out of society for his unethical conduct, longed for nothing more than the destruction of that society which had rightly ostracized him.

'If we keep this up long enough,' he said to Andrews when they were discussing the matter in Andrews's office on the day of the great 'dissemination', 'we can destroy the whole social fabric of the country. We can make it rotten from the inside, and the whole damned lot will come down round everybody's ears — and I don't have to tell you that the collapse of an ordered society means plenty of pickings for those who are waiting. What do you get after an earthquake or a major catastrophe? You get looters, and that in a sense is what we can be, because we shall be level-headed where everybody else will not realise what has happened.'

'Sounds reasonable,' Andrews admitted. Though even he was a trifle uneasy at the immense scope of the idea. Findon had no such misgivings: he was a far better judge of the average man and woman and what makes up the structure of so-called civilised conduct than Andrews was.

The first results of this indiscriminate vibratory dissemination became evident a few days later, when no less than six daily papers found themselves in a deluge of libel suits. The reason being that the editors were, for once, printing the truth about everything. The real, unvarnished truth. For long they had proclaimed in their leading articles that they spoke nothing but the actual facts, but they always refrained from saying that the actual facts were, to say the least of it, twisted and turned very slightly to make them palatable for human consumption.

Now there were no punches pulled. This or that famous character was ruthlessly pilloried, libelled, vilified, and even insulted without any attempt to gloss things over. No newspaper can speak of public personalities in the way that these six particular newspapers did, and even the editors themselves did not realize what had happened. They certainly did not know that they had come under the influence of the projectors, even though they realized that they were finding it absolutely impossible to say anything but the truth. Either in their business lives or in their private lives.

And the newspapers were not the only ones involved. There were the smaller but just as important incidents. There were dozens of cases where doctors told the truth to their patients, and were promptly almost put on trial for what appeared to be a complete breach of ethics. Then again there were the amazing interviews on radio and television wherein the interviewers asked such personal questions and received such staggering answers that in the case of television that much overworked notice from the early days of broadcasting: 'Normal service will be resumed as soon as possible' was used almost constantly. In fact, in all the major public fields, there was absolute chaos. Everybody was walking on the quicksand of unexpectedness, not knowing what was going to happen next and wondering what mysterious thing had occurred to so upset the normal balance of life.

6

Carson Intervenes

'Why doesn't someone do something about it?' asked Ethel Carson of her husband one evening when they were together in the lounge.

It was rare for them to find a chance to be together. Up to now Dr. Carson had spent every evening in his laboratory or else lecturing. But on this particular occasion he seemed inclined to take a rest. Bobby, as usual, was out with Betty.

'The answer to that one, my dear,' Carson said, sighing 'is that nobody can do anything. The police have tried and you know what happened to them. In fact the police are still trying and getting nowhere. Why? Because every one of them has a secret he doesn't wish exposed, and therefore self-preservation being the dominant instinct that it is, it's better to let the thing go on than find oneself in an utterly indefensible position. I don't blame any of the policemen — I'd do the same myself in their place.'

'But the evil is growing,' Ethel insisted, spreading her hands. 'Mark, you just can't sit there and let things go on. First it was blackmail, we know that from the papers, and now it's increased in all directions. We have the newspapers involved, the doctors, the big politicians, radio, television! Where on earth is it going to finish? And incidentally, I thought you said that if your Lie Destroyer appeared in any way publicly you were going to bring an action. You surely can't want anything more public than this?'

'That was before it dawned on me that the police much prefer to keep quiet than to take action.' Carson gave a weary smile. 'So much belongs to everything, my dear. One has to move with circumstances. And I must say that I am pretty astonished to learn to what uses the Lie Destroyer can be put.'

Ethel moved restlessly.

'None of which answers the point,' she insisted. 'What are you going to do?'

'Nothing. There's nothing I can do.'

'But are you sure? What about that new apparatus you are building in the laboratory? Frankly, Mark, I can't see the point of it. Isn't there enough trouble with these Lie Destroyers — I assume there must be quite a lot of them now — without you making another one to add to the difficulties?'

'I'm not working on a Lie Destroyer,' Carson replied slowly. 'Nor have I been from the very commencement. I only made one of them, and that was the one that was stolen. This fresh apparatus is something very different.'

'Very different!' Ethel echoed. 'Why? What is it? Don't tell me it is something as outlandish as the Lie Destroyer. I couldn't stand that!'

'No. Nothing like that. It is an apparatus for mass hypnotism!'

This time Ethel could only stare.

'It can control not only one person, but hundreds, thousands at a time. It's simply a matter of amplifying thought waves and that's not particularly difficult. Just as one can amplify the waves of sound so one can amplify the waves of thought.'

'But what's the use of that?' Ethel demanded. 'It's the Lie Destroyer that we're worried about. You fool around in the laboratory making an apparatus to hypnotize people. What do you suppose would happen if these crooks got hold of that? They'd have an even higher time than they're having now.'

Carson only smiled. It was plain that there was some pretty deep secret at the back of his mind . . .

And under the direction of Andrews and Dr. Findon things went on apace.

'We did very nicely out of our last three-fold onslaught,' Andrews commented, when he had called a special conference at his saloon office. 'From all accounts there is absolute confusion and chaos within the three twenty-mile radii in which we worked. Naturally we shan't have to repeat the attack in the same place again otherwise there's likely to be trouble, so we'll move on to the next spot. And something occurs to me, Findon,' he added, glancing at the scientist. 'Is it possible for Scotland Yard men with detectors to trace where our vibration is coming from?'

'Scientifically,' Findon answered, 'nothing is impossible, but I don't doubt that some of the backroom boys at the Yard will in time devise a means of detecting where our apparatus is working. Our only way of defeating that is to keep constantly on the move and never repeat an attack twice in one spot. It shouldn't be difficult to handle because we only operate for something like fifteen minutes all told from one particular location. And that won't just give the Yard boys any chance to catch up with us.'

'Seems fair enough,' Andrews admitted. 'All right, now to the reason for my calling you all together here.' He glanced round on the various scientific experts and the head men who controlled the three different areas or rather bases up and down the country. 'We know now that we have more or less got England where we want it,' Andrews said. 'And though we're not making at the moment any great financial gain from the chaos, we shall as time goes on. For the present tendency seems to be — even as Dr. Findon said it would — for society to start crumbling at the roots. When everybody speaks the truth everybody is afraid of each other. Of how much they know. I think that it's time we went after bigger game.'

'Meaning?' Findon asked, raising his eyebrows.

'Well, why do we stop in England?' Andrews asked. 'We've got the whole world that we could deal with, and I can think of lots of juicy places where we could probably extract a tremendous amount of money — the United States for instance. I don't doubt there are plenty there who would pay a good deal to keep quiet!'

'Gangsterism on a world-wide scale?' Findon asked, grinning. 'Well, it suits me. I've no particular reason to love society either on the other side of the Atlantic or on this one. What do you propose?'

'I propose that several of our picked men here should go abroad and study out the possibilities. Bases can be erected there, just as they have in England here.

By degrees we can pretty well cover the whole Earth. There's no reason why not. It will, of course, take a considerable time to master America, for we can only use a twenty-mile radius at once, and that seems to be our limit. It will take us maybe years to cover the thousands of miles of territory which there are in America.'

'Doesn't matter how long it takes,' one of the men said. 'Just so long as we do it. We've made a good beginning; there's no reason why we shouldn't keep on going.'

So they talked back and forth, these men planning gangsterism on a world-wide scale. As Andrews had remarked, they had not, at the moment, made any tremendous return from their activities; that would come later, when constant unrest and each man's fear of his neighbour would cause a shattering of the social fabric of civilisation. That must inevitably come for when no secret is safe, when anybody is liable to blurt out some of their most precious knowledge at a moment's notice anything can happen.

And there was no doubt that there was tremendous unrest. And it grew every time the projectors were set to work from a different position. Doctors found themselves personally attacked for having dared to state openly their patients' cases. Politicians were thrown out of office by the clamourings of their electors, simply because it was realized that they were not as they had presented themselves to be; and as for what was happening behind the scenes of radio and television, this was nobody's business. Big names were disappearing like trees in a bushfire, and the extraordinary thing was that in every instance it was those men and women who had styled themselves as such purists were now being exposed as almost the biggest villains in the community. The amazing somersaults and reversals that Carson's Lie Destroyer brought to light were positively breathtaking.

Scotland Yard was, of course, deeply interested in what was happening. The Assistant Commissioner, however, responsible to the public, could not let things go on as they were. Realizing that this was no ordinary police job he called in his back-room boys, those scientists without whom

Scotland Yard could hardly operate under modern conditions.

'Something scientific somewhere is at the back of all this,' the Assistant Commissioner declared when his men were gathered in the office to hear what he had to say. 'It is not my province to deal in scientific things, but you men ought to be able to get to the root of it. Dr. Sheldon, have you any ideas as to what might be happening?'

'None,' Sheldon replied. He was one of the foremost scientists of the Yard. 'As a matter of fact, sir, I haven't paid any particular attention, beyond noticing that there is a great deal of blackmail going on and that an almost inconceivable number of people are finding it very awkward insofar that they are now telling the truth constantly for perhaps the first time in their lives. Usually one only associated consistent truth-telling with those in the religious orders. When the average man and woman states outright exactly what he or she thinks there is obviously something in it. As to whether that something is scientific, I wouldn't know.'

'It can't be anything else,' one of the other men said bluntly 'But how to find it is the problem.'

'Well find it we must, no matter what,' the Assistant Commissioner said bluntly. 'The public is looking to us to do something and that means that we've got to do it. Remember that we are only the servants of the public when we're finished.'

'I could more easily imagine trying to catch the east wind in a bottle,' one of the scientists commented. 'I've studied these incidents very carefully, chiefly for the scientific interest of the thing. It seems to me that suddenly whole areas of the country, extending to a perimeter of about twenty miles, suddenly becomes truthful. That, of course, can't happen without there being some predisposing mental cause.' He frowned pensively.

'I think we can throw hypnotism overboard as the reason, particularly as it seems to be permanent, once it has arrived, which brings us back to an electrical emanation of some kind. The only possible way is to use electrical

164

detectors, and see if we can get a reading.'

'Yes, but how?' Sheldon demanded. 'From all accounts these happenings occur at different places every time. How are we to know where it's going to happen next? Going round with a detector is no use whatever. Not unless we have some really sound idea as to where things are going to happen. Or better still, who is at the back of it all.'

The Assistant Commissioner pondered for a moment and then asked a question.

'To trace the cause of this trouble, if it was electrical, would it require a special instrument? A different one from what we usually use?'

'Well, no,' Sheldon replied, considering. 'It seems to me that if the trouble is electrical an ordinary electrical detector will do the job. But it won't show us exactly what the trouble is; only where the source of the trouble is.'

'Then in that case, there is one particular move we can make,' the A.C. decided, looking somewhat relieved. 'We have any number of these ordinary electrical detectors. I think that every police headquarters in the country should be supplied with one.'

'Every one!' Sheldon exclaimed, astonished.

'Every one,' the Assistant Commissioner insisted. 'They must be kept watch upon constantly, and as soon as there is any deflection on any of these detectors we must be instantly notified. We shall know that trouble in that particular case came from that area and from that we may be able to make a move.'

The Assistant Commissioner's plan was, of course, quite unorthodox, but then so was the situation, and he was prepared to go to any length to try to get things under control. Accordingly, in response to his orders electrical detectors were dispatched to all the chief police headquarters in the country, with strict instructions that observations must be made upon them day and night, no matter what. Immediately there was any sign of any reaction, Scotland Yard must be informed.

This was the only move the Yard could make at the moment; as to what would happen afterwards, well, that would come when there was a report from somewhere.

Meanwhile Andrews and his men were also at work. Those particular men whom Andrews deemed suitable were dispatched abroad with orders to make the necessary contacts with those of their own fraternity — that is to say those known to be more or less against the law yet working just within it. In a word, men who would be willing to risk anything to throw in their lot with the Lie Destroyer gang.

America, Canada, and most of Europe were therefore combed by Andrews's agents, whilst on the other hand Dr. Findon made arrangements for the 'underground' manufacture of further projectors. This was going to be a worldwide scheme. Those behind it could see no end to the possibilities, and certainly they did not for a moment ever believe that the law could catch up with them. They were perfectly sure that, if things came to the worst, they would be able to turn the tables even as Andrews had turned the tables upon the unfortunate Inspector Houghton.

It was nearly three weeks after the general installation of detectors at police headquarters up and down the country before there came an emergency call to Scotland Yard. It came from the Bedford region, and therefore was obviously within the southern area of the crooks' activities. The message was brief, but the inspector at the other end stated that his detector showed distinct signs of oscillation under a very strong electrical influence, and that he himself had just discovered that he was unable to speak anything but the truth.

The Assistant Commissioner wasted no time. He gave orders for the Bedfordshire police to use every available man to search for anything unusual, possibly a mobile van, within a twenty-mile radius. Meanwhile, Scotland Yard experts which included several scientists, flew by fast plane from London.

When they arrived in Bedfordshire they found that the police there had as yet not discovered anything, but this did not deter Dr. Sheldon, in charge of the operations, who immediately went to work with his own men to thoroughly study the area.

It was whilst they studied the area that the people within it had all found themselves suddenly bereft of the power to tell untruths. And as had happened in so many cases, so it happened in theirs. There was a repetition of the old suspicions, the squabbles, the insults, even open fighting amongst the lower classes — all the general upsets produced by this sudden complete reversal of normal human behaviour.

Six hours searching by Sheldon and his experts failed to discover any sign of the cause of the trouble, but they did discover the tracks of what appeared to be some kind of brake or Army van — the tyre marks being quite distinctive — leading across a deserted field. They followed it in high hopes only to discover that it disappeared on the roadway.

Later investigation showed that within twenty miles of these tyre tracks the tendency to truthfulness was obvious, therefore it seemed a fair assumption that this van or truck, or whatever it had been, had been the prime centre of the disturbance. But where the van had gone now, or how possibly to locate its journey, was the problem.

In fact at this point the matter was really out of Sheldon's hands, so he handed it over to the normal Yard officials for investigation. And they pursued the matter to the best of their abilities, making all possible enquiries. They were diligent and thorough, and as is often the case, diligence and thoroughness finally brought a reward, though it was six days later before this happened.

By then each man had learned enough to pool his information with the others, and from various witnesses on the road and from the houses fronting the road, they had gleaned enough evidence to note that a large green enclosed van, using the Army type tread of tyre, had been observed going along the road, and it had appeared that its journey had finished at a Candyfloss factory situated on a deserted site between two housing estates.

So far, so good. But this did not prove anything. The Yard was not so incautious as to suddenly plunge into inquiries. What they did do was to carefully investigate the ownership of the Candyfloss factory, and after they had discovered all that was needful they placed their findings before the Assistant Commissioner for further directions.

'The trouble is,' the Assistant Commissioner said wearily, 'the whole thing may be circumstantial. We don't know that this truck that has been observed really was the one that caused the trouble, although all the evidence seems to point to it. Apparently the owner of this Candyfloss factory is somebody by the name of Clifford Andrews.'

'Clifford Andrews!' repeated Dr. Sheldon, looking up sharply. 'Why I seem to remember something in connection with him. Let me see now, what was it?' Since he failed to immediately bring it to mind, the only thing he could do was make a search of the record department. Finally his browsing through the various files was successful. He returned to the Assistant Commissioner's office after about twenty minutes, a folder in his hands.

'I thought the name Andrews was familiar,' he said, seating himself again and scanning through the file's contents. 'Some four years ago he was mixed up in a scientific case — that is if it is the same Clifford Andrews, and I shouldn't be at all surprised — and he only just escaped a very long sentence. Even as it was he got a year in jail. It seems to suggest to me that we're certainly on to the right person. If he went wrong once it seems an almost inevitable law that he would go wrong again.'

'Yes, that's all right,' the A.C. agreed, 'but the point is: how are we to get at them? We can't prove anything. We never saw the van in action; we only know that there was an electrical reaction on the detector; which we assume came from the source of whatever is causing the present truthfulness. Before we can do a thing we have got to have proof, and the problem is, how to get it.'

There was silence for a while as the scientists considered, then the A.C. asked another question.

'You have all the particulars about that

172

detector, Sheldon. Is it possible to tell from it what kind of an electrical apparatus is being used?'

'Quite impossible,' Sheldon replied. 'I've studied the report which was given to me by the Bedfordshire police and I've taken away the instrument which acts in a stop-watch fashion. All it does show is that the electrical energy being generated is of tremendous voltage, far more so than one normally gets. It had swung over the detector's needle to the absolute maximum scale reading, a most unusual thing. It suggests that there was as much energy in the emanation being given forth as there is in a normal low-powered radio station, but as to the nature of what was being given forth, we have no clue whatever.'

The Assistant Commissioner got to his feet in exasperation. 'There must be somebody who can help us in this matter. I know that you gentlemen are doing your best but maybe this calls for someone who has specialised. Have you any suggestions? Some expert whom we might call in who's not even connected with the Yard?'

'If it is a matter of radio and electronics, you can't do better than ask Dr. Mark Carson,' Sheldon said, shrugging, not in the least troubled by professional jealousy. 'I have had plenty of dealings with him in the past in matters of electronics, and he certainly knows his business. He might be able to make a few suggestions.'

The A.C. nodded, wasted no more time, and lifted the telephone. Within a few minutes he had been put through to Carson's home to be informed that he was away at his normal governmental place of business. Not that this deterred the A.C. He asked for the number where he could get Carson, and after another ten minutes was speaking to him on the line.

'Is it coincidence, or what, that has led you to me?' Carson asked, when he had been told the particulars.

'No coincidence about it, doctor,' the A.C. replied. 'It seems that one of our men, Dr. Sheldon, seems to recall you helping him in the past, and — '

'Oh, yes, of course,' Carson interrupted. 'Sheldon, eh? Yes, I know him well. Well, what in particular do you wish to know?'

'It's about this sudden truthfulness that seems to be afflicting everybody,' the A.C. explained. 'We believe it might be some kind of electrical or electronic equipment which is causing it, but we're hamstrung in trying to get to the root of the problem. Do you think you could help us?'

Carson laughed shortly. 'Do I think I could help you! Dammit man, I invented the thing, but I'd given up all hope of trying to get any sense out of Scotland Yard. They've already had one try and not managed to do anything.'

'One try?' the A.C. echoed. 'This is the first I've heard of it — Look, doctor, this is too important to discuss over the telephone; can you come over?'

'Er — yes. I'll come over right away,' Carson assented. 'I'm not particularly needed at the moment. I'll be right with you.' He rang off. The A.C. also put his telephone down and sat back with some relief.

'Anything doing, sir?' Sheldon asked.

'Definitely. Carson's going to come over right away. I really think we have something now, gentlemen. It will interest you to know that Dr Carson invented this Lie Destroyer, or so he says. And he also says that he has asked the Yard to try and put things straight but nothing was ever done. I just wonder where that comes in? I certainly have not any report about it.'

'He invented it?' Sheldon repeated, amazed. 'But he must know what's going on! Why on earth hasn't he come out into the open and said something about it?'

The A.C. shrugged. 'Don't ask me. Maybe he'll be able to explain that more clearly when he gets here.'

In three quarters of an hour Carson had arrived. He was shown into the A.C.'s office, nodded briefly to the assembled men, then took the chair that was proffered him.

'Sorry to have to call you off your work like this, doctor,' the A.C. apologized, 'but we thought that you might be able to help us. Since mentioning over the telephone that you invented the Lie Destroyer, there is of course, no doubt about it whatever, I suppose,' the A.C, asked, sitting down again, 'that you really meant what you said?'

'But of course I did.' Carson looked surprised. 'You don't suppose that I make statements just for the fun of it, do you?'

'No, no. Of course not.' The A.C. cleared his throat. 'However, it is certainly an immense advantage that you know all about it. It means that I don't have to explain anything. We're absolutely up against it, doctor. The public is demanding action and we just don't know how to get any. We've got a certain distance but that's all.'

'That machine was stolen from me in the first place by one Clifford Andrews,' Carson said.

'Ah!' Sheldon exclaimed, his eyes brightening as he glanced towards the file that he had brought in. 'I was right. I'd just worked out the fact that Andrews was responsible for everything, but what we have got to have is proof.'

'Exactly,' Carson acceded dryly. 'That is what has been holding me up, too. Without proof we can't do a thing.'

'According to our investigations,' the A.C. continued. 'Andrews is running a

Candyfloss factory. In fact, several such factories. As far as we can make out they're quite legitimate business concerns, but it seems more than obvious that they're just blinds for his real purposes.'

'Yes, obviously,' Carson assented. 'Some little time ago I came to the Yard here and put things in the hands of Inspector Houghton — '

'Oh, yes. Houghton,' the Assistant Commissioner interrupted. 'He committed suicide not so long ago. The reason was obscure. Still, there it is, just one of those things.'

'The reason was not obscure to me,' Carson said. 'He committed suicide because he came under the influence of the Lie Destroyer. There must have been some very deep secret in his life which he was afraid would be revealed. There could be no other reason for his committing suicide as he did,'

'Personally I feel almost responsible for his death. That is one reason why I have not approached the Yard again, in case other inspectors happen to suffer the same fate. I don't want that kind of thing on my conscience. But you can't mean, Commissioner, that you don't know about the Yard having investigated? They've made several attempts and each one has failed.'

'Oh, yes, I know of the trifling efforts we have made,' the A.C. agreed, looking rather abashed. 'What I mean is that I was not aware of this particular instance to which you refer. About your tackling Houghton. So that was the reason for his suicide,' he broke off, musing.

'Well, it doesn't concern us now,' Sheldon put in briefly. 'What we've got to do is get at Andrews, and the quicker the better. What are the facts, Dr. Carson? You invented the machine. What happened then, what are its possibilities, what can it do?'

Carson wasted no time in explaining every detail, including the story of the theft of the machine. Naturally he did not explain that Bobby had been directly responsible for the machine's theft. He simply made it appear that Andrews had done it off his own bat — which in truth he really had.

'To know what the machine can do,' Carson finished, 'and to prove that these men are actually doing it and in control of everything is the problem. We have got to catch them red-handed, so to speak, and we can be mighty sure that they won't give us an opportunity of doing that.'

'On the other hand,' the A.C. said, 'we just can't sit here and wait for pennies from heaven. We've got to make some sort of a move. We know where they are. What is to prevent us from going right in and arresting them on a charge of suspicion? We have that right, anyhow.'

For quite a long time there was silence in the A.C.'s office. Every eye was fixed on Carson as he sat thoughtfully considering the problem. At last he looked up.

'I think, gentlemen, that no matter what you do you will not find it possible to get at these men, they have everything too well organised. And Clifford Andrews is surely a man who knows every trick on the board. Believe me, since my machine was stolen, I have done little else but try to devise ways and means not only of getting the machine back, but of bringing to book the men who stole it. And, I *have* such a scheme.

'Mind you, Scotland Yard will come into it, but not in the normal way of things. By that, I mean, I don't expect the Yard to march in and do the usual melodramatic arrest business. No. I want them to remain in the background and do exactly as I suggest.'

'Well, we're willing to listen to any reasonable scheme,' the A.C. assented promptly. 'I only hope that it is not one that will take a long time to develop. I hardly need to add that the public is vilifying us pretty well, especially through the newspapers, and in those areas where truth is rife they're certainly not pulling their punches any. In fact we are made out to be about the biggest dopes in Christendom.'

'You cannot get at men like these by ordinary police methods,' Carson explained. 'It has to be something scientific. A scientific invention was the cause of the original theft, as we know, and I believe that a scientific method can also bring them to absolute defeat. I was intending to come and have a word with you Commissioner about a point that is actually a technical law question.

'Obviously we cannot pin these men down without absolute proof. Now, if you knew exactly what these men were going to do, if we had a confession in their own words or at least a statement made undeniably by one of the leaders of the gang, would that be accepted as evidence?'

'Most certainly it would,' the Commissioner replied. 'That's just the kind of proof we're trying to get. And we cannot see any conceivable way of doing it. Why, have you a method?'

'I think so.' Carson smiled tautly. 'Remember, gentlemen, my stake in this is much bigger than anybody's. It is my invention that is causing all this trouble. The very last thing I wanted — and for that matter the very last thing I ever expected. Now listen carefully, gentlemen, to what I have to say. It is essential that you grasp the idea in its full implication, and I warn you it will not be easy for those of you who are not scientists to grasp what I'm driving at. It is the only possible way in which we can uproot this evil which has come into our midst — '

7

The New Machine

When he arrived home that evening after
his usual date with Betty, Bobby was very
much surprised to find his father awaiting
his arrival in the lounge. It was unusual in
that his father usually spent every evening
in the laboratory, sometimes till well after
midnight. Certainly he never seemed the
least concerned what happened to his
son, unless he happened to be unusually
late; then of course it was pure, parental
ire that led him to await Bobby's arrival.
This time it could not possibly be that,
Bobby decided, for it was only half-past
ten.

'I would like a word with you, Bobby,'
Carson said briefly. 'It can either be now
or after you've had supper, whichever you
please.'

'Then make it now,' Bobby said. 'I
don't think so well after supper; that is

granting it is something I shall have to think about.'

'There is no doubt about that,' Carson answered. 'You can hear it here just as well as anywhere else. It doesn't matter your mother knowing because I've already explained it to her.'

'Explained what?' Bobby took a seat in the armchair and looked at his father in puzzlement.

'I think,' Carson said, 'that the time has come, Bobby, when you can make reparation for the very wrong thing you did in agreeing to accept money from Clifford Andrews for my invention. But for that unhappy incident he would never have managed to steal the Lie Destroyer. Everything that he learned from you on that evening was the direct contributory cause of the machine being stolen. Now has come the opportunity for you to make amends.'

'Oh, I see.' Bobby looked uneasy. 'What does this mean — that the police are going to take action or something?'

'No, nothing like that. The police have nothing to do with it — at least as far as you are concerned. No, this is a totally different thing altogether. I want you to get in touch with Clifford Andrews again.'

'What?' Bobby stared blankly. 'After all that's happened you want me to start doing that?'

'Yes, because you're the only person in close contact with me who possibly can. He'll be less suspicious of you than of anybody, because he knows that you are willing to sell out. Or at least, that you were. That he double-crossed you on the first occasion won't matter in this instance, or at least it won't have to. The fact remains you are the best person to handle the matter I have in mind.'

'Really, Mark,' Mrs. Carson protested. 'I do wish you would stop working out these involved plans. Before you've finished you're going to get poor Bobby into an awful mess.'

'And if poor Bobby doesn't do something nobody else can,' Carson snapped. 'I can't think of anybody better to do this job. Not only because Andrews is quite likely to listen to him, but also because I still think that you, Bobby, owe me some kind of return for the most reprehensible way in which you behaved.'

'Well,' Bobby sighed. 'What do I have to do? Walk into the lions' den and declare what?'

'I want you to walk into the lions' den, yes. But the reason will probably surprise you. You are going to offer to Clifford Andrews another scientific machine, infinitely more dangerous than the one he has already stolen. If I'm anything of a psychologist, and I think I am, I'm pretty sure that he will jump at the opportunity.'

'But that's crazy,' Bobby protested, rising to his feet in amazement. 'Hasn't Andrews done enough damage already? Aren't things going from bad to worse? Why, even in Throgmorton Street there are financiers giving up business because of the way things are going on, and I know quite a lot of solicitors' firms who are — '

'Please let me finish,' Carson interrupted acidly. 'I know exactly what I'm doing, and everything is in connivance with Scotland Yard. I have been there today and have had quite a long conversation with the Assistant Commissioner and his scientific squad. You have nothing to fear. You have the law on your side, and if it makes you feel anything of a hero, everything depends on you. All this country can be saved from the depredations of the Lie Destroyer, or rather the depredations of Andrews, if you do exactly as I instruct.'

'Well, I feel anything but a hero,' Bobby said uneasily. 'And don't forget that I have the constant Achilles Heel of being forced to tell the truth if I'm asked a direct question.'

'Not necessarily,' Carson replied. 'You have enough control over yourself now to keep your mouth shut if you're asked an awkward question. See that you do. But I don't think in this instance you will be asked any awkward questions — However, to get back to the point. You are going to sell the idea to Cliff Andrews, which it will be worth his while either to buy or steal — in the first instance I should try and get him to buy — an apparatus for producing mass hypnosis.'

'For what?' Bobby asked weakly. 'I said

this was crazy before — now I'm sure of it. Hand an instrument like that to Cliff Andrews and what in the world is going to happen? You don't seem to realise what kind of a man he is, Dad! He's completely without scruples — he's already shown that. With an instrument like the one you suggest, well, we might as well give up the ghost and stop thinking anything further.'

'If you've finished,' Carson said irritably, 'I will continue. Now, I have been working on this instrument for several weeks now. You have seen me at it in the laboratory; so far, you have understood the instrument to be a new Lie Destroyer — but it is nothing of the kind. I'm not going to construct another Lie Destroyer, because I mean to get the original one back, and have all the duplicates and large-size models of it destroyed. No. This is something very much more complicated and very much more dangerous. Let our friends have it. I have a very definite reason for doing so. Once they have got it in their hands I have every reason to believe that it will prove their undoing.'

Bobby was not exactly a fool in spite of his youth, but for the life of him he could not see how such an instrument could possibly be anything but a most frightful menace. Nevertheless he dared not say any more, not with his father's steely eyes fixed upon him.

'All right,' he said finally, 'so I try and sell the idea to Cliff Andrews. And suppose he doesn't fall for it?'

'He will,' Carson said confidently. 'You can't offer a man like that such a terrific weapon and expect him to turn it down. He'll buy it all right. First thing in the morning I want you to go and see him — er — yes, being Saturday you should be able to manage it.'

'Yes, all right,' Bobby assented, for he did not go to the office on Saturday. 'I'm quite willing. Do I take the instrument itself or a sketch plan, or what do I do?'

'I want you to take the instrument itself. It is not a particularly big thing as you are already aware having seen it. No larger than a portable radio. You will tell Andrews that you have appropriated it, and that you're reasonably sure that I will not notice its disappearance. You will also tell him that you have seen it in action, and that it does actually do what is claimed of it — in other words produce hypnosis of any number of people within an area of two miles.'

'And if he asks me to demonstrate it on the spot, what am I supposed to do? I'm no scientist, Dad.'

'You will refrain from doing anything like that. You will have an easy get-out by saying that you are not a scientist and don't understand how it works. But you do know that it does work. That will be quite sufficient for Andrews. He'll keep the machine and he'll probably have his scientific expert examine it before anything is done.

'That is nothing more than I expect. You'll have to remember, Bobby, that you must not make any attempt to try and operate the machine. Leave that entirely to Andrews's experts. All you have to do is sell him the idea. After that I have a fancy that many things will happen.'

'Yes, I'm afraid they will,' Bobby agreed gloomily. 'Within a very short time practically the whole of England will go under the sway of hypnotic power, unless I miss my guess.'

Carson smiled enigmatically. 'Well, we'll see about that. Anyway, those are all the instructions that I can give you. It is up to you to do the rest. You'll do it?'

'Yes, I'll do it,' Bobby agreed. 'As you say, I owe you some reparation for the way I behaved, though I must say I don't feel at all happy at going into Cliff Andrews's den. Anything might happen to me if he decides to get tough.'

'Andrews,' Carson said, 'is not just the common type of criminal, the everyday killer — he's an extremely clever organiser and is interested only in mass effects. He won't do anything in the lines of murdering you or trying to beat you up — of that I'm quite sure.'

'Well, I'm glad you are,' Mrs. Carson said uneasily. 'Personally, I think you ought to be ashamed of yourself, Mark, for ever making such a proposition at all.'

'I'm not ashamed of anything,' Carson replied brusquely. 'I'm trying to get an effect and I don't care how I get it. If my own son has to be used as the cat's paw, very well, he has to be used, that's all there is to it. This business has got to be stamped out, and Bobby here is the only one who can possibly do it.'

After which nothing more was said — and the following morning, with considerable trepidation, Bobby set off on his mission. His father, knowing from previous experience that Andrews would not be at the poolrooms, gave Bobby the saloon owner's private address. In consequence, Bobby arrived there towards ten o'clock, and the rather fox-faced manservant looked at him in some surprise. There were many callers at the Andrews residence, but very few as youthful as Bobby.

'My name's Carson,' Bobby introduced himself. 'Bobby Carson. I don't think you'll know me, but I must see Mr. Andrews. Most important.'

'Have you an appointment?' the manservant asked, coldly.

'No. No appointment. Just tell him that I have something scientific here which I am convinced will interest him. I think he'll see me then.'

'If you'll just step inside, young man, I'll enquire if the master is at home.'

Bobby obeyed and walked into the hall, there remaining while the butler moved silently into the more distant regions of the residence.

After a while he returned.

'The master is still at breakfast, Mr. Carson, but he will nonetheless see you, if you will step this way to the breakfast room — '

Bobby followed meekly behind the tall austere figure, and was presently shown into a comfortable room where Andrews was seated alone at breakfast. That there had been somebody else there — probably his wife — was shown by a half-eaten breakfast at the other side of the table and a chair hastily pushed aside.

'I'm not going to say that this is a pleasure,' Andrews said dryly, 'because it is not. What do you want, young Carson? Make it short, if you please. I have a lot of business on hand.'

'I think you will delay it long enough to hear about this.' Bobby held up the instrument in his case that he was carrying. 'Although our last deal went completely haywire somewhere and you cheated me out of five thousand pounds, I still don't like my father's scientific inventions.'

'Well?' Andrews asked. 'So you propose doing what? If you've come here to threaten me, you'd better think again. I'm in no mood to stand for — '

'I'm not here to do any threatening,' Bobby said, seating himself. 'All I want to do is to try and interest you in something scientific — this.' Again he held up the case.

'What the devil is that?' Andrews asked impatiently.

'As far as I understand it, it is a machine for producing hypnosis. It doesn't just hypnotize one person — it can deal with dozens at a time and make them do whatever the operator com-mands.'

Andrews did not say anything. He finished his breakfast, sat reflecting, and then got up from the table. Lighting a cigarette he began to pace around slowly, clearly weighing things up. Bobby almost knew what he was thinking. He was wondering if this was some kind of snare, set by Dr. Carson himself.

'This isn't a trick,' Bobby said frankly, taking the plunge. And in this he spoke the absolute truth. For it was not a trick — it was a deliberately-laid scheme, and Bobby, as far as he knew, was doing exactly as he was told. His inability to tell a lie made it that he could not do anything else but the right thing insofar as he knew it. But how far it corresponded with the actual facts was debatable. Only his father knew of the real issues behind the scheme.

'All right, since you can't tell a lie I'll take your word for that,' Andrews said. 'So this machine produces hypnosis, does it? Where's your proof of that?'

'The only proof of that I have is that of seeing it in action.' Here again, Bobby was not telling a lie. He was only repeating the statement that his father had told him to make.

'You've seen it in action, have you?' Andrews' eyes pinned Bobby from the further end of the room. 'When and where? How many people?'

Bobby was silent. He could not answer this question truthfully, so instead he switched on to another of his father's statements.

'It can hynotise almost any number of people up to a distance of about two miles. Of that there is no possible doubt. What my father plans to do with this machine I don't know. But I do know that I am not interested in anything he does that's scientific, and that my main ambition in life is to get my own back on him for the thing he did to me when he stopped me telling untruths.'

'If you stopped talking in a roundabout way, maybe we could do business,' Andrews said curtly. 'If that machine is all that you claim for it, I could certainly do something with it. What are you doing, offering it to me or do you want to sell it or what?'

'Naturally I want to sell it,' Bobby replied frankly. 'You did me out of five thousand pounds for that Lie Destroyer and I kept my mouth shut ever since where I could have got you into hot water as you probably realized, so how about five thousand pounds again? This time to keep my mouth shut and take this invention as well.'

'And what happens when your father discovers that this invention has disappeared from his laboratory?' Andrews questioned.

Bobby shrugged. 'It will have to be explained away as thieves, that's all. If he directly questions me I shall keep silent. But I don't think he will question me — nor do I think he'll miss this instrument. I know exactly what I'm doing. It's either for you to take the plunge or leave it alone. I know plenty who'd like an instrument like this — it's even more powerful than the Lie Destroyer in the things it can do. Or probably you have realized that?'

'I'm realizing quite a lot of things,' Andrews responded, 'but I wish I could rid myself of the overriding suspicion that this whole business is a trick.'

'I can only repeat that it is not a trick,' Bobby replied. 'And that is the absolute truth. I don't have to tell you again that I can't help but tell the truth, do I?'

'All right,' Andrews decided, his curiosity and avarice overriding his normal level-headedness. 'I'll take a gamble. You let me have that machine and you can have five thousand pounds in cash. A cheque wouldn't be safe for either of us.'

'Suits me,' Bobby assented, and placed the machine on the corner of the breakfast table. 'I don't know how it operates,' he continued, 'but I do know what it can do. You'll have to have one of your own scientific men to examine it before you start meddling with it.'

'I'll do that all right,' Andrews answered briefly. 'Come with me and I'll fix you up with that payment.'

Andrews led the way out of the breakfast-room across the hall and into his study. Bobby followed him dutifully and stood waiting and watching while Andrews opened the wall safe and proceeded to extract a steel cash-box.

From it he counted out five thousand pounds in high value notes and handed them over. There was no hesitation about his action — this was one of those cases where he could attempt no jiggery pokery, and he knew it. In any case if the invention was worthwhile — and there was little doubt in his mind that it probably would be — five thousand pounds was a small sum to pay for it. On the other hand if the instrument proved to be useless then the five thousand pounds would have to be put against the original five thousand that he had managed to avoid paying.

'Thanks,' Bobby said briefly. He counted the notes for his own satisfaction, then stuffed them in his pockets. 'I don't intend to contact you again, Mr. Andrews. And I need hardly add that it would be wisest that you don't contact me, but you'll find that I haven't sold you a pup.'

'For your own sake you'd better not have,' Andrews said curtly.

'All right! Thanks! And good morning!'

Bobby wasted no time in leaving. He only began to breathe freely when he was a mile away from the Andrews residence. He returned home to make his report to his father. Carson listened in attentive silence, and when Bobby had related everything that had happened his father gave one of his rare chuckles.

'Couldn't be better,' he exclaimed. 'My boy for once in my life I'm proud of you. By your courage in performing this action you may have saved tens of thousands of men and women in this country from all kinds of blackmailing activities — in fact more than that — you may have laid the whole blackmailing gang by the heels.'

'I'll be hanged if I can see how?' Bobby sighed. 'Honestly Dad, I just don't get it. How can a machine for producing hypnosis bring down this blackmailing empire of which Andrews is the leader?'

'You just let me worry over that, my boy. You've done your share — the rest is up to me and Scotland Yard.'

So with that Bobby had to be satisfied. Carson, however became a man of great activity from that moment onwards. Apparently there was some kind of subsidiary apparatus connected with the hypnotic equipment, for from the steel safe Carson produced some extremely complicated-looking equipment housed in a glass case, and once again looking very much like a radio set in construction. With this instrument he went immediately to Scotland Yard and sought an interview with the A.C, Dr. Sheldon, and the other backroom boys.

'My son has done his share,' Carson announced with a certain paternal satisfaction. 'I may as well confess gentlemen, that I almost thought that he would not fall in with the idea. However, he evidently has more courage than I gave him credit for, and he has sold Andrews the idea that he now has a machine for producing hypnosis. The rest is up to us.'

'If it works,' Sheldon said doubtfully, and Carson gave him a bitter look.

'Dr. Sheldon, I should have thought that you would know by this time that I don't waste my time working on inventions that do not show a result. It will work all right — the only point is when? Anyhow gentlemen, I'm handing over to you the other part of the equipment upon which you will have to keep constant watch.'

'We'll do that all right,' Sheldon said.

'The only thing bothering me is — what happens if Andrews and his men should move away from their London base? If they should go to the Midlands or the North we'll be completely lost. We're not likely to get any reactions from those distances, are we?'

'No,' Carson admitted, 'but I hardly see why they should leave the centre of their web which is definitely down in London here. Apparently their headquarters vary considerably but I have made allowance for that. Whether they meet at Andrews's actual residence, at his saloon, or at the Candyfloss factory we shall still be within range at Whitehall here. I led my son to tell them that the range of the instrument is two miles. Actually it is nearer two hundred, but that is beside the point. All we have to do now is wait for a reaction. And I'm extremely sure that we shall get one — '

Meanwhile Andrews was in action. Since his personal supervision was not required any longer in the matter of Lie Destroyer machines — his various agents all having their instructions as to how to

203

proceed — he could devote his time to this new scientific machine which had come into his possession. He went to his saloon headquarters, checked upon the usual normal day's business, and then drove on to his Candyfloss factory.

Here, as he had expected, he found Dr. Findon at work in the so-called sweet-testing department, at the back of the factory. More correctly this sweet-testing section was a scientific laboratory, but cleverly disguised so that any sudden arrival by the police would not reveal its true purpose. Findon was at work on some obscure experiment when Andrews entered carrying the hypnosis machine in his hand.

'If you have a moment, doctor,' Andrews said quickly, 'I believe we've got something here that will absolutely put us on top of the world — and it was that young idiot Carson again who put it right into my hands.'

Findon looked up sharply, his lean, acid face obviously startled. 'Young Carson! For that reason I wouldn't trust any of it. Good God, man, you haven't been such a fool as to accept anything from him, have you? You might know that it must be a trick.'

'Under ordinary circumstances I probably would regard it as such,' Andrews admitted, looking indignant at the fact that his acumen should be questioned, 'but don't forget that young Carson is incapable of lying. The cross-questioning I gave him satisfied me that the whole deal was perfectly genuine. Anyway it's worth a chance. And here's what this instrument can do.'

Andrews gave a detailed description of the instrument's possibilities as Bobby had outlined them to him. Findon listened to him intently, meanwhile taking the lid from the instrument and gazing at its radio-like outlines.

'Sounds reasonable,' he admitted, when at length Andrews had concluded. 'I suppose you want me to make a thorough analysis to make sure that young Carson was speaking the truth?'

'Naturally,' Andrews replied. 'I'll leave it to you. As soon as you've finished your examination let me know what you think.

If this works out it's the most marvellous thing that ever dropped into our hands. What puzzles me is why Dr. Carson even invents such marvellous equipment and then never seems to use it. Well, not to any great extent, anyway. All that does seem to happen is that his son steals them and hands them on to us. A most extraordinary state of affairs.'

'And one which, somehow, I don't trust,' Findon said thinking. 'I'm sure there's something peculiar about all this somewhere. Anyway I'll have a look at this equipment and see whether it lives up to its reputation.'

Satisfied with this Andrews took his departure and Findon wasted no more time in dismantling the plastic cowling from the apparatus and commencing a detailed examination of its internal workings.

It was late that evening when he went over to Andrews's saloon, finding him as usual in his private office.

'As far as I can tell,' Findon said, 'the instrument you asked me to examine is all that young Carson claims for it. It definitely is built to handle the control of thought waves! I've analyzed that fact very carefully, and there can be no doubt about it. Not having any human subject who was willing to fall under the influence of amplified hypnosis, I tried the effect on several laboratory specimens, notably mice, and that tame monkey that we keep for occasional research experiments. They did exactly as I told them obviously controlled by my mind. All I had to do was set the amplifier to full, concentrate into the electromagnetic absorption device within the mechanism and the thing was done.'

'Which means,' Andrews asked eagerly, 'that mass hypnosis can be accomplished?'

'I should say that there's not the least doubt of it,' Findon answered. 'Before we actually use it though on a big scale that is, we must certainly try a human being somewhere. Any suggestions?'

Andrews grinned a little. 'There's one person who always seems to do the dirty work around here, Findon,' he added, 'and that's Arthur. I should think he might make a very good victim.'

'I don't agree,' Findon replied. 'Arthur is a man of rather low grade intelligence. To hypnotize him even in the ordinary way would not be a tremendous accomplishment, and to do it with amplified apparatus simply wouldn't tell us anything. What we require is somebody who is known to be very strong-willed; and if they break down under it then the thing is worth bothering with.'

'All right,' Andrews said cheerfully, 'I'm never afraid to take a chance. How will I do?'

'Excellent,' Findon agreed, slowly. 'I have the equipment outside. I can bring it in and try it right away if you like?'

'Suits me, all right. But are you quite sure you can get me out of it once you have got me into it? Remember I just can't sort of remain hypnotized after the thing has been done.'

'You needn't worry about that,' Findon answered briefly. 'There's a device on the apparatus which neutralises the effect produced. There's no doubt about it, you know,' Findon said as he moved towards the door, 'this man Carson is an absolute scientific genius. Pity is that he doesn't seem to realize it. Anyway, I'll be back in a minute.'

Findon departed to return within a few minutes carrying the apparatus in his hand. He set it on the desk, removed the lid, then pushed in the power-plug into the skirting board socket.

Andrews remained in his swivel chair, watching; a vague uneasiness crossed his face as he saw the nose of the equipment, which looked rather like an elongated funnel with a lens at the end, pointing straight at him. Findon took up a position behind the equipment.

If he had spoken the truth Andrews would have liked to have backed out right now. He did not trust Findon for one thing, and suppose this instrument were just another Lie Destroyer in disguise? If that were so and Andrews found himself under its influence he would lose everything that he had fought for. Everything depended on whether Findon was playing the game straight or not. In any event Andrews didn't dare to argue with him so he sat tight and waited for something to happen.

'Simplicity seems to be the keynote of this apparatus,' Findon said, snapping on a button, and immediately there was the whirring of the internal workings. 'There's nothing difficult to understand. You switch on, you concentrate into this magnetic plate here, you set the pointer to the required distance, which at the moment happens to be four feet — your distance away from me — and then plunge over the master switch thus.'

It clicked over into place under the scientist's lean hands; the whirring ceased, presumably as the whole of the power was transferred into the output side of the equipment.

Andrews still sat waiting but within seconds he felt the tremendous impact of Findon's thoughts. It was as though he were receiving irresistible commands and no matter what efforts of will he himself made he was quite powerless to assert himself in any way.

He lifted a paperweight and threw it

into the wastepaper basket, then he rose from his swivel chair and turned the chair upside down on the floor, he sat deliberately on the window ledge and even went to the length of performing a hornpipe. He was perfectly conscious of doing all these things and yet no effort of his could prevent him doing them.

And suddenly there was a faint whirring within his head, or so it seemed, and he was back to normal, looking at Findon smiling sardonically over the top of the apparatus.

'See what I mean?' the scientist asked cynically. 'Literally, Andrews, you danced to my tune. And everybody else can dance to the same tune as well — to any tune we choose to play! It's the greatest thing that ever happened.'

'Well, I'm satisfied,' Andrews said, obviously somewhat shaken. 'This thing apparently has a range of two miles, or so young Carson said. Do you think we can improve on that?'

'I imagine so, by increasing the output side and building bigger machines. That I can easily do. Or at least I can draw the

necessary sketches and have our manu-
facturers do the rest. With this and the
Lie Destroyer there's nothing to prevent
us having humanity eating out of the
hollow of our hand in no time.'

'Yes,' Andrews agreed slowly. 'How
long do you think you will be before you
get the first of these machines off the
production line?'

'Well, probably in about a week at the
rate we can do things these days. The
actual design isn't complicated, as I said
at first. That's one advantage about
Carson — he doesn't make things too
impossible to follow. Well, have I to go
ahead?' Findon asked, closing the lid on
the apparatus.

'As far as I'm concerned, the sky's the
limit as usual,' Andrews replied. 'Let me
know when you have something definite
to report — '

Meanwhile the Lie Destroyer was being
used exactly according to plan. In some
ways it was doing good. In certain parts
of Europe for instance, where there was a
considerable amount of international
tension, this tension was being lessened

by the agents of Andrews.

They, getting to know the secrets of the opposite side through the operation of the Lie Destroyer, were putting one man against another and not staying with the small fry but operating directly with the high-ups. And when high-ups are in possession of each other's deepest secrets and military intentions, there no longer is any point in trying to be secretive or in bargaining for an ideal political position.

Thus it was that a mysterious wave of friendship spread over the formerly suspicious protagonists in the political scene. But this was about the only good side to the Lie Destroyer. In other countries it was, as Andrews had calculated, doing a great deal to undermine the social security of several nations. With the passage of more months, if the thing went on unchecked, an absolute collapse of society as understood by the average man and woman was inevitable. Andrews, however, was the kind of man who, having a new toy to play with, was liable to neglect the old one. Therefore he left the management of the Lie Destroyer to his various agents, and instead waited impatiently for news of the production of mass hypnosis machines on a large scale.

Indeed he could better understand the powers of mass compulsion through amplification than he could the scientific ramifications of the Lie Destroyer.

Meanwhile, in the scientific division at Scotland yard, the companion apparatus to the hypnosis machine, which Dr. Carson had delivered with the instruction that it was to be watched night and day, was still standing motionless, giving no readings. But a fortnight later there was a sudden change. The reaction meter began to operate. Immediately the plan that had been decided upon was put into action.

Carson was notified and asked to come over to Scotland Yard right away — which he did. He found Sheldon and the other scientists all in the laboratory, their attention centred upon the companion apparatus to the hypnotizer.

But they were not so much looking at the recording instruments as listening to a loudspeaker immediately over their heads.

From it, not entirely clear, but nonetheless audible, were coming words, which words were being taken down on closely approximated tape recorders.

'Hello, Carson,' Sheldon said briefly, looking up. 'It seems to be working. You'd better take a seat, and listen to this. It's been very interesting up to now, and from the sound of things it may get even more interesting as it goes on.'

Carson, knowing exactly what to expect, did not speak, and so interrupt the continuity of words coming from the speaker. Instead he silently seated himself and listened with the others. The voice that presently came from the speaker sounded very much like Andrews — except that it had a peculiar woolly quality. It was a voice, and yet not a voice. There was a strange, disembodied effect about it, as though it did not really belong to him. Nonetheless, what he said was distinct enough.

'To my mind, Findon, the first thing we must do is deal with England. You say that you've increased the radius of the hypnosis apparatus from about two miles to fifty by building bigger machines? Well, we can do a lot within an area of fifty miles, especially if we operate in the heart of London. Which brings me to the same point again. Do you think that as in the case of the Lie Destroyer, this instrument is capable of being detected by the Scotland Yard scientists?'

'That I can't say.' Findon also sounded peculiarly remote and far away. 'Maybe a detection is possible — they're no fools at Scotland Yard and they have instruments which could make us pretty uncomfortable, but by and large I imagine that once again the speed with which we operate and then move on will be sufficient to keep us on the safe side.'

The A.C., who was among the scientists, looked up sharply.

'What more do we need than that?' he asked quickly. 'That's a direct confession in itself as to what these men are up to.'

Since nobody answered him, and also because he had absolute jurisdiction in the matter anyway, he lifted up the telephone.

'Give me Richards,' he ordered briefly,

and within a moment or two he added: 'All right, Richards, go to it. Follow that detector beam, which you must have by now, to its source and arrest the men at the other end. Bring them in.'

The A.C. put the telephone down again. The scientists looked at each other, smiling slightly, and Carson was smiling the widest of all.

The biggest surprise came to Andrews and Findon seated in Andrews's back office in the saloon when two Scotland Yard men walked right in upon them without so much as a knock.

'What the devil's the meaning of this?' Andrews demanded, when the chief inspector had identified himself with his warrant card. 'By what right do you come barging into here? Don't you realise that this amounts to trespass.'

'You're under arrest,' the chief inspector answered curtly. 'Here's my warrant.' He held it out.

Andrews just stared. For that matter so did Findon. His eyes moved to the hypnosis equipment on the table — the original machine that Bobby Carson had brought — and then he looked back at the Yard men. There was something peculiar here, but he — Findon — could not quite put his finger on it at the moment.

Certainly no time was wasted. With the authority they possessed the Yard men hustled both Andrews and Findon out of the office and into the waiting patrol car.

Ten minutes later they were at Scotland Yard. They were not immediately docketed and officially charged, instead they were led to the laboratory regions where Carson, Sheldon, the A.C. and the remaining scientists were still assembled in one of the main sections of the laboratory.

'I don't know what kind of an idea this is,' Andrews said impatiently when he and Findon were shown in. 'Seems to me, Commissioner, that you're going to have a lot to answer for. I thought you knew better than to pick up innocent citizens without a good deal of proof.'

'It so happens,' Carson said, rising, 'that we have all the proof we need, and you two have supplied it, though it is quite possible that you are not aware of having done so.'

Andrews looked blank. 'What in the name of the devil are you talking about?' he demanded.

'Just this.' Carson gave a signal and the tape recording equipment, which had taken down the voices from the speaker, began to play back from the very beginning.

In stunned amazement Findon and Andrews listened until finally there was a click and the recording ceased.

'But this is impossible,' Findon cried. 'You could not possibly have had a concealed microphone in Andrews's office, I know that because the place was constantly guarded, and always before we discussed anything we searched for the possibility of a hidden microphone or any police trick. And yet here, through this speaker, obviously having been taken down by the recorder, is a conversation between Andrews and myself.'

'Yes,' Carson agreed. 'And do you admit that the conversation is exactly as it took place?'

'Well, almost,' Findon said slowly, as

Andrews gave him an angry, bewildered look. 'We didn't quite speak in those words. That is to say, the sense of the questions and the answers is more or less exact, but I'm prepared to swear that our actual words were not the ones that the tape recorder has taken down.'

'No, they weren't,' Carson assented, with still that bland look of satisfaction upon his face. 'What actually happened my friends is, the machine recorded your thoughts, and we picked them up. Now, when you say anything you naturally have to think of it first, but not always does the statement you make absolutely follow the mental arrangement of it, which you have beforehand. You think of a question and it naturally forms into words in the only language that you understand. But when you utter if with your tongue, it might undergo slight variation even though the sense of the thing is the same. Do you follow me?'

'I'm damned if I do,' Andrews declared furiously. 'What kind of blasted scientific jiggery-pokery do you call this, anyway?'

'It is not jiggery-pokery,' Carson

assured him, 'it is just science applied to the highest degree, namely, to the mental realm. To put it more clearly, my friend, you were sold a machine that was supposed to be for hypnosis. And to a certain extent that was correct. I took that risk. It can produce hypnosis, but its radius is nearer two hundred miles than two miles.'

'But I examined that machine,' Findon interrupted, 'and I found that it applies solely to mental waves.'

'Naturally,' Carson assented, grinning. 'But in two senses. You only saw the obvious means, which was just as I thought you would do. You saw that it could produce mass hypnosis, but you did not also see that for a distance of maybe six feet it can also pick up the thoughts of anybody and retransmit them along the hypnotic beam. Naturally, only such a thing could happen when the apparatus was in action. I assume that you had this apparatus in action this evening?'

'Yes, we did,' Andrews agreed. 'We were going to try an experimental hypnosis.'

'Yes,' Carson said, 'and at that time, while the apparatus was switched on, though not actually emanating an hypnosis, you asked each other these questions which have been recorded.'

'Right enough,' Findon agreed, beginning to grasp the scientific point.

'Well, there you are then.' Carson spread his hands. 'The apparatus picked up your thoughts and retransmitted them over a distance of two hundred miles, and here in Scotland Yard we had the necessary special receiver to pick up those thought vibrations. Believe me, at other times when you had the instrument switched on for hypnosis we have also picked up your thoughts, but they were not in any way useful to us. That is to say they were not condemnatory in any sense, nor could they be construed as legal proof of your recent activities. But tonight the particular questions which you asked each other, and gave each other answers, provided all the evidence that we need.'

'What this means, then,' Andrews said bitterly, 'is that you sent your son with a supposed hypnosis machine, whereas you did it because it could transmit our thoughts? And you knew that at some time it would give us away by revealing what we were thinking?'

'Exactly. I did not wish to record the audible voice — in fact I could not because I knew you were too wary to let a microphone be slipped within your province — so I resorted to this method of picking up thoughts and having them transmitted and having them received by scientific apparatus. There's nothing you can do about it, gentlemen,' Carson said. 'This is the only machine in the world so far, to the best of my knowledge, which can pick up thoughts and permit of them being transcribed back into sound.'

Findon, not in the least disturbed by the fact that he had been caught out, was if anything fascinated by the scientific implications.

'To my mind,' he said frankly, looking at Carson, 'this thought amplification instrument is about the biggest masterpiece you've turned out. And though it may have caught me on the hop I congratulate you upon it. What I cannot quite see is how it transcribes thought into audible sound?'

'It is not difficult,' Carson replied, willing as usual to explain the scientific issues to a fellow scientist no matter on what side of the fence they stood. 'You know the old fundamental law which transcribes sound into light, as in the case of a sound track on the side of a film? Well, this is merely the same process carried a few degrees further.

'Thought waves are emanated electrically, and anything electrical can be transcribed into any of the basic electrical forms. It could be transcribed into light, it could be transcribed into sound. In this case it was transcribed into sound. The only necessity is the right kind of transformer, which upon receiving the minute impulses created by thought, builds them up electronically into a different pattern. A vibratory pattern. And vibration can be turned into sound without the least difficulty. They could only follow their original pattern, therefore they followed the outline and the language which has been in your mind. The result was an apparent voice, but blurred and peculiarly indistinct because

224

it was a mental medium in the first place and not an actual oral one.'

'Well,' Andrews said frankly, 'I'll be damned. There's nothing more I can say.'

'That's where you're wrong,' the A.C. commented, 'there's a great deal more you can say yet, Andrews. And when you come into court you're going to. Meantime, all this rotten empire that you've built up from the Lie Destroyer and all the blackmail and the villainy and the thieving, that is all going to be pulled down within a few days. Dr. Carson here took a chance that your giant hypnosis machines would go into action before we got the evidence we wanted from the smaller most essential machine, but his gamble came off, and you see where you find yourselves. And believe me, this is where you're going to stop.'

THE RATTENBURY MYSTERY
CLIMATE INCORPORATED
THE FIVE MATCHBOXES
EXCEPT FOR ONE THING
BLACK MARIA, M.A.
ONE STEP TOO FAR
THE THIRTY-FIRST OF JUNE
THE FROZEN LIMIT
ONE REMAINED SEATED
THE MURDERED SCHOOLGIRL
SECRET OF THE RING
OTHER EYES WATCHING
I SPY . . .
FOOL'S PARADISE
DON'T TOUCH ME
THE FOURTH DOOR
THE SPIKED BOY
THE SLITHERERS
MAN OF TWO WORLDS
THE ATLANTIC TUNNEL
THE EMPTY COFFINS
LIQUID DEATH
PATTERN OF MURDER
NEBULA

We do hope that you have enjoyed reading this large print book.

Did you know that all of our titles are available for purchase?

We publish a wide range of high quality large print books including:
Romances, Mysteries, Classics
General Fiction
Non Fiction and Westerns

Special interest titles available in large print are:
The Little Oxford Dictionary
Music Book, Song Book
Hymn Book, Service Book

Also available from us courtesy of Oxford University Press:
Young Readers' Dictionary
(large print edition)
Young Readers' Thesaurus
(large print edition)

For further information or a free brochure, please contact us at:
Ulverscroft Large Print Books Ltd.,
The Green, Bradgate Road, Anstey,
Leicester, LE7 7FU, England.
Tel: (00 44) **0116 236 4325**
Fax: (00 44) **0116 234 0205**

Other titles in the
Linford Mystery Library:

CALL IN THE FEDS!

Gordon Landsborough

In Freshwater, Captain Lanny was an honest cop with problems: his men and his chief were on the take from the local gangster Boss Myrtle. Bonnie, Myrtle's daughter, was in love with Lanny, but he couldn't pursue the relationship because of her father's criminal activities. Lanny's problems multiplied as Freshwater became threatened by an influx of murderous criminals from New York — a gang of bank raiders, and Pretty Boy, a psychotic murderer of young women. Then Bonnie went missing . . .

THE EDEN MYSTERY

Sydney J. Bounds

Interstellar entrepreneurs, the Eden clan, had opened up new planets, building a galactic empire, governed by the United Worlds' Federation. However, stability is threatened by an impending war between the worlds of Technos and Mogul. The Federation fears intervention by the clan's sole survivor, Kyle Eden. Meanwhile, Hew Keston is investigating the Eden family's history for the media corporation Stereoscopic Inc. But his life is in danger — someone is stopping him from learning the secrets of the Eden clan!

THE LOST FILES
OF SHERLOCK HOLMES

Paul D. Gilbert

Dr John Watson finally reopens the lid of his old tin dispatch box and unearths a veritable treasure trove of unpublished tales recounting the remarkable skills of his friend and colleague, Mr Sherlock Holmes. With the detective's consent, we are now finally privileged to witness how Holmes, with his customary brilliance, unravelled the secrets lurking within a too-perfect police constable, a Colonel with a passion for Arthurian mythology, and the public house which never sold a single pint of ale . . .